Henry Atlee Ingram

The Life and Character of Stephen Girard

Henry Atlee Ingram

The Life and Character of Stephen Girard

ISBN/EAN: 9783337416218

Printed in Europe, USA, Canada, Australia, Japan

Cover: Foto ©Raphael Reischuk / pixelio.de

More available books at **www.hansebooks.com**

THE LIFE AND CHARACTER

OF

STEPHEN GIRARD,

OF THE CITY OF PHILADELPHIA,
IN THE COMMONWEALTH OF PENNSYLVANIA,

MARINER AND MERCHANT.

WITH

AN APPENDIX DESCRIPTIVE OF GIRARD COLLEGE.

BY

HENRY ATLEE INGRAM, LL. B.

———

PHILADELPHIA, PA.:
E. STANLEY HART, 321 CHESTNUT STREET.
1884.

TO THE

DESCENDANTS IN AMERICA

OF

Jean Girard, de Mombrun,

THIS BIOGRAPHY OF HIS BROTHER STEPHEN IS, WITH
THEIR PERMISSION, RESPECTFULLY INSCRIBED

BY

THE AUTHOR.

PREFACE.

I
N presenting a new biography of Stephen Girard
the writer has considered that a few words in explanation of the various reasons prompting his work
may not be amiss, and as these reasons are best set
forth through a short consideration of already existing
memoirs, it is proposed here briefly to refer to the
latter.

The first attempt at a biography of Girard closely
followed his decease in 1831, being the work of
Stephen Simpson,[1] a former clerk in Girard's Bank,
whose probable motives in its conception and production have been elsewhere adverted to in the body of the
present work. It is sufficient here to say that this
narrative shows such garbled, perverted, or wantonly
misstated facts that a mere casual reference to its
inconsistencies and flat self-contradictions will perhaps
quite fully justify the re-presentment of the subject
in a more reasonable light. But its author has gone
further, and, not hesitating to rely upon himself where
his investigations failed to supply the desired material, has produced a work whose inaccuracy and

[1] *Biography of Stephen Girard.* By Stephen Simpson. Philadelphia, 1832.
Reprint, King & Baird, 607 Sansom Street, Philadelphia, 1867.

patent malice is the more regrettable since it contains otherwise sufficient truth to have naturally formed the basis of the majority of subsequent sketches. Its author has himself confessed that, save for the generally known acts of Girard's life, he has chiefly relied upon public gossip,[1] although he usually fails to mention his authorities, and elsewhere uses liberally his position of clerk in the Bank to lend a factitious importance to his work as the personal observations of one in close daily contact with his subject. The present writer is indebted to the oldest living apprentice of Girard for the statement that at no time did anything approximating an intimacy exist between this clerk and his employer, and that the light esteem openly evinced by the latter for his subordinate wholly limited their infrequent communications to such matters as arose from the affairs of the Bank.[2] It will be easily apparent, therefore, owing to the short time spent daily by Girard in his Bank, that this clerk's opportunities for acquiring accurate information of his employer were even more scanty than those of the counting-house apprentices, to say nothing of his own admission that having upon one occasion had the impertinence to question Girard upon his private life, he met with a complete rebuff.[3]

[1] Preface to Simpson's *Biography of Girard*, p. 5.
[2] Professor William Wagner, Lecture IV.
[3] See article in *American Daily Advertiser*, Philadelphia, Jan. 12th, 1832.

"Any one," says Professor Wagner in his first lecture upon Girard, "who will read this biography of
Mr. Girard, which I thus publicly pronounce a tissue
of lies, sticking out on every page, will perceive that
the whole account is embittered and venomous, and
that the author has tortured his imagination to find
an opportunity to falsify and pervert. Now, before
dilating upon it, let us inquire for a moment who this
biographer was. When the charter of the old Bank
of the United States expired and Mr. Girard purchased
the building, establishing in it his own Bank, he
appointed George Simpson, the cashier of the former
institution, to the same position in his new concern.
Stephen Simpson was the son of this latter, and, with
Mr. Girard's consent, was appointed by his father to
the situation of clerk in the Bank, in which position
he continued until the death of his father. Stephen
then aspired to the cashiership that his father had
held, but, unfortunately for him, Joseph Roberts, the
first teller, stood between him and the coveted office.
Mr. Girard had confidence in Roberts, but very little
in Simpson, the result being that the former received
the appointment, and the latter became thereupon the
uncompromising enemy of Mr. Girard."

This feeling of resentment having been reinforced
by the punishment of a reduction of salary upon the
occasion of Simpson's assault upon a fellow-book-

keeper in the Bank,[1] "every invention of fancy and perversion of facts has been resorted to by him to injure the reputation and tarnish the fame of that benevolent man;—with which statement before you, for the truth of which I vouch, can you expect a calm or dispassionate narrative from a biographer so influenced? As well might you expect clear water from a muddy pool."[2]

But, unfortunately, the keynote struck by the general tenor of Simpson's book has been patently followed by Girard's subsequent biographers, with one notable exception; these writers, most of whom were contributors to periodical literature, finding it much easier to publish excerpts from that remarkable production than to investigate the subject for themselves. From these circumstances, together with the possession of documentary evidence, referred to in its place, and consisting of baptismal records and sworn testimony refuting many of that author's statements, the present writer regards the works of Simpson and his followers as utterly unreliable. And though in the present work the former has, nevertheless, been frequently referred to, and even quoted freely, it will be found that the references are wholly to facts likely to have come under that author's personal notice, being matters of common report, of which his book forms a

---

[1] Post p. 135.   [2] Professor William Wagner, Lecture I.

convenient record, or else comprise reluctant admissions in Girard's favor. These latter have been quoted without reserve, in the belief that favorable statements by an adverse party form strong evidence in their subject's behalf, the present writer especially desiring to call attention to the fact that in many cases the passages flatly controvert the statements of other portions of the book itself.

The notable exception among Girard's biographers referred to above is Henry W. Arey, formerly secretary of Girard College, who, having free access to the papers stored at the College, impliedly protests against the false inferences drawn by Simpson, and presents in his own sketch a fair picture of Girard as he actually appeared to his fellows.[1] To this sketch the present writer has great pleasure in acknowledging his indebtedness; and though the possession of certain documents and evidence not at that biographer's disposal compels him to differ from several of the latter's conclusious, he recognizes everywhere the author's endeavor to present his facts with the strictest impartiality. But, unfortunately, having depended mainly upon a journal kept by Girard, commencing in the year 1774,[2] this author, like the others, has relied for information as to Girard's origin upon common report

---

[1] *Girard College and its Founder.* By Henry W. Arey. Phila., 1860.
[2] Arey, p. 8.

or the earlier work of Simpson, and has, consequently, committed the same error of ascribing to his subject that exceedingly humble parentage which forms one of the salient defects of the earlier biographies.

How such a report can have originated is beyond the power of the present writer to explain, but it will be seen by the evidence herein presented that it must have been the invention of absolute ignorance, if, indeed, the public is not additionally indebted for it to Stephen Simpson, among whose other malicious stories it first appears. The present writer has, however, no desire to enter into controversy with regard to this or any other of the statements in the following pages, it having been his endeavor in every case to convince solely by the presentation of well-attested proofs, believing that the surest argument than can be advanced is the simple statement of facts he is in a position to support. He is aware of the objections to be urged against that minute consideration of Girard's domestic life which he has permitted himself in the second part of the present work ; but while admitting that such investigation of petty detail is often liable to do injustice to character at large, he has felt the necessity of stating openly and accurately the intimate facts of a life which has been already grossly misrepresented, and finds his chief excuse for so doing in the remarkable success with which his subject's character withstands the trying ordeal of such scrutiny.

Conscious of many defects in his presentation of the subject, he lays claim to no merit of literary workmanship, but is quite willing that whatever value may be attached to this biography shall rest entirely upon the validity of the various documents already several times mentioned, which documents are now for the first time at the disposal of a biographer of Girard, and which are as follows :

(1.) A copy of the official record of Girard's birth and baptism, certified under their respective seals in 1857 by the Mayoralty of Bordeaux and the United States Consul at Bordeaux, France, to be used as competent evidence in the various suits brought by the heirs against his estate.

(2.) The sworn testimony taken in France under a commission from the United States Circuit Court for the Eastern District of Pennsylvania[1] for the same purpose.

(3.) The lectures upon Girard, delivered by Professor William Wagner, the MSS. of which has been placed without reserve at the present writer's service, and whose great value arises from the fact that from the year 1810 to the death of Girard, Professor Wagner

---

[1] See *Transcript of the Records of the U. S. Supreme Court,* "Vidal *vs.* The Mayor, etc.," No. 22, Vol. II, page 85 of *Transcript* and p. 120 of the case.

was in most confidential relations with him, first as
his favorite apprentice, and afterward acting as his
agent in all parts of the world.

(4.) The traditions in the family, comprising
inter alia the substance of the present writer's many
conversations with the three nieces of Girard, daughters of his brother Jean, who lived in the Water
Street mansion from their early childhood to the
death of Girard, and who were present during the
whole of the latter's illness, as well as at his death.
The writer has had access to the MSS. notes left by
the youngest of these nieces, Henriette Marie Girard-
Clark (Vve. Lallemand), to which he is greatly indebted for many of the observations upon Girard's
domestic life.

(5.) A "Memorial of Stephen Girard against
Joseph Baldesqui," in Girard's handwriting.

(6.) A great number of French letters, written
to Girard by his father, his two brothers, and his
sister, covering a period of thirty-one years from
1772 to 1803, and comprising his intimate correspondence during the whole period, of which no
information has heretofore been accessible to any
biographer.

The writer, having submitted his completed work
to Professor Wagner, founder of the " Wagner Free
Institute of Science," has the pleasure of subjoining

the following letter from the only business associate of Girard now living:

HALL OF THE WAGNER FREE INSTITUTE OF SCIENCE, }
PHILADELPHIA, April 26th, 1884. }

HENRY A. INGRAM, ESQ.:

My Dear Sir:—I have carefully considered "THE LIFE OF STEPHEN GIRARD, MARINER AND MERCHANT," as he was always wont to be called, which you have submitted to me for my opinion before publication. I may safely say that I fairly consider myself in a position to criticise closely any matters relating to my old master, the great Girard, owing to my long and intimate knowledge of him, extending over a period of twenty-one years from the time of my first being apprenticed to him to the day of his death. I heartily and unhesitatingly approve of the work which you have done, and feel delighted that so correct a biography is to be presented to the world. I believe it to be strictly correct, so far as the facts are concerned, and, what is more, to be the first true biography published of my old master, which does honor and justice to his true char- acter as an earnest, philosophic, and philanthropic man.

I am, my dear sir, yours very truly,

WILLIAM WAGNER,
President and Founder of the Wagner Free Institute of Science.

STEPHEN GIRARD.

" On regardait chez moi par les fentes, et l'on me calomniait ; j'ai ouvert portes et fenêtres, afin qu'on me connût, du moins, tel que je suis."

  —J. J. ROUSSEAU, in Souvestre's *Un Philosophe sous les Toits*.

PART I.

STEPHEN GIRARD, the eldest son and second child of Pierre Girard and of Anne Marie Lafargue, his wife, was born on the 20th of May, 1750, in "a three-story brick house in the old Philadelphia style"[1] in the Rue Ramonet aux Chartrous, near the City of Bordeaux, France, and was baptized in the Roman Catholic faith the following day, having for godfather Etienne Foiesse, and for godmother Anne Lafargue, the sister of his mother.[2]

The house, which was surrounded by quite a plot of land, had probably been purchased by Pierre Girard about the time of his marriage with Made-

---

[1] Notes of Henriette Marie Girard-Clark (Vve. Lallemand).
[2] Officially certified copy of baptismal record of Stephen Girard.

moiselle Lafargue, and upon his decease it was inherited by Stephen, who in turn devised it to his brother, Etienne, and his niece, Victoire Fénélon, in equal moieties.[1] It thus became the homestead of several generations of Pierre Girard's descendants, for the former was not himself a native of Bordeaux, but of the little city of Périgueux, in the Dordogne. Many generations of the family had resided in this latter city, being widely known for their devotion to the sea, upon which they had been engaged from time out of mind, either commercially or in the service of the Royal Navy. It was a family well known and heartily respected, of considerable wealth—Pierre Girard and his brothers having inherited several ships from their father—and whose social position had just been additionally well established by the conferring upon Pierre Girard of the Cross of the Royal and Military Order of Saint Louis.

The circumstances which gave rise to this last honorable distinction are so curtly narrated upon the official Register of Marriages at Bordeaux on the occasion of Pierre Girard's marriage to Mademoiselle Lafargue that the present writer feels justified in quoting the extract in full. Unfortunately he is unable to give the exact date of this latter ceremony,

[1] Will, Article IX.

but it probably followed close upon the occurrence mentioned below, which took place when Pierre Girard was but thirty years old :

"*In 1744 France being at War with the English, Pierre Girard finding himself upon the Squadron at Brest, the English sent a Fire Ship into the [midst of the] Squadron, which set on Fire a Vessel of Line.*

"*M. Pierre Girard fired with Zeal for his Country, by his Skill and Vigilance succeeded in Extinguishing the Fire and Saved the Ship, which the Flames would have Destroyed, which Vessel in a few Days was in Condition to Rejoin the Squadron. His Majesty, Louis XV, having Learned of the Heroic Action which M. Pierre Girard had done, Knighted him, and Ordered a gold Medal to be Struck, which He gave to Pierre Girard as a Badge of Honour, and that his Name Should be Placed on the Inscription of the Registers of the Admiralty of Paris, to Engrave in the Hearts of his Family, the Memory of their Ancestor.*"[1]

It should be added that according to the rules of the Order the honor of knighthood could not be conferred upon any save a naval or military *officer*,[2] showing that Pierre Girard already occupied a position of some distinction, a circumstance which may

---

[1] "Extrait des Actes de Mariage" déposé aux Ecritures de M. Patotte Notaire, Rue St. Rémy, Bordeaux, France.

[2] Clark's *Concise History of Knighthood*, London, 1784, Vol. I, p. 235; Perrot's *Collection Historique des Ordres de Chevalerie*, etc., Paris, 1820.

account for the multiplication of rewards mentioned in the quoted extract.

Born of this line of seafaring men, Stephen Girard early showed a marked predilection in the same direction, but he was kept at home acquiring such elementary education as was possible in France one hundred and twenty-five years ago, the thoroughness of which rudimentary training became apparent in his later completion of certain studies unaided.[1] It had been his father's hope and intention that all his sons should enter a professional life, and it is possible that this might have been the result in Stephen's case had not an accident during his eighth year summarily broken off his attention to his studies—an attention the consequent long indulgence of his preference for open-air life found him very unwilling to renew.

This accident was the loss of his right eye, the result of throwing wet oyster-shells upon a bonfire, the heat of which splintering the shells, a fragment entered Stephen's right eye, at once destroying the sight in it beyond the hope of restoration. The grief and pain attending the catastrophe was heightened by his playmates' subsequent thoughtless ridicule of his altered face, leaving so great an impression upon the sensitive young lad's mind that he vividly remembered it to the day of his death. As a consequence,

[1] Compare Arey, p. 7.

he withdrew almost wholly from their society, occupying himself with that of his brother Jean [de Mombrun], an early intimacy between the two brothers being thus commenced that lasted, with but one interruption, during the long period that stretched to the death of the younger. This friendship forms the brightest thread in the whole fabric of the elder brother's life, and was of equal warmth on the part of both brothers, a happy result of the patient care with which their mother had sought to render her family a unit, and one the more worthy of remark when it is remembered that to all other persons the elder showed an exceedingly undemonstrative disposition. His reserve of character was no doubt rendered somewhat morbid by the comparative isolation to which his proud and sensitive temper had relegated him, and it is curious to consider the influence such a trivial and childish circumstance as his playmates' ridicule had in the after-development of his life, for it is doubtless to this event may be fundamentally traced that distrust of, and semi-contempt for so many of his fellows which he later displayed; and the disposition whose most salient feature became its self-reliance and complete indifference to the cavil or judgment of his neighbors was primarily dependent for its direction in not a small degree upon this very circumstance of its original exceeding sensibility.

Although, as has been said above, Stephen was
carefully drilled in such elementary studies as are
commonly pursued by a lad of eight years old,
there can be no doubt that he was not naturally
studious, and a sympathy for his misfortune having
permitted great latitude in his preference for out-
door life, his later studies soon came to occupy by
far the smallest part of his attention. He possessed
excellent faculties of observation and a very reten-
tive memory, supplying in a great measure the
routine work of the school-room, and there can
be no doubt that at the time he was not at all
averse to escape from the uncongenial labor of the
latter. It is in the injudicious indulgence of this
preference upon his part that is to be found the
explanation of the neglect with which upon one
occasion he reproached his father, the consciousness
of his loss having led him, in 1813, to write the
following letter, which a consideration of the fore-
going remarks will show was decidedly unjust:
"I have the proud satisfaction to know that my
conduct, my labor, and my economy have enabled
me to do one hundred times more for my relatives
than they all together have done for me since the
day of my birth. While my brothers were taught
at college, I was the only one whose education
was neglected. But the love of labor, which has

not left me yet, has placed me in the ranks of citizens useful to society." [1]

In the mere amount of money expended this statement was probably true. But it is the start in life which is most difficult to get, and for this Stephen was indebted to his father, notwithstanding the rather ungracious manner in which he had recognized his relative's subsequent claims upon him. But the stress under which this letter was written [2] was sufficient to excuse it in a great measure, the more so as it is the only time he gave vent to his feelings in this manner, and the tone of conscious strength in it is certainly to be pardoned one who had indeed almost literally " made his way alone with means gained from his nurse, the Sea." [3]

From his earliest childhood Stephen had been remarkable for precocious dignity and grave self-assertion, and with these masterful traits was coupled a passionate and rather domineering temper, which, when opposed, was displayed with considerable violence. His mother was still earnestly seeking to modify this character, so directly opposed to the usual careless high spirits of young French children, and to teach him the necessary self-control, when her death, which occurred while Stephen was yet

[1] Arey, pp. 6 and 7.   [2] The capture of his ship, the " Montesquieu."
[3] Arey, p. 7.   Letter written in 1789.

quite a young lad, found him with the lesson still un-
learned. The considerable influence which, as eldest
son, he doubtless wielded in the immediate family
after his mother's death, probably fostered the independence of character already natural to him, and
his impatience of discipline, speedily reasserting its
mastery, grew in time to be not only the most fruitful
source of the unhappiness of his after life, but also
the proximate cause of his leaving his father's home.

Not that he was at all unhappy at this period, however, for during the few years following his mother's
decease no untoward event marred the peace of the
family circle, and probably none would have arisen
had not Pierre Girard selected a second wife in the
person of Madame Giraud (*née* Lachapelle), an American or West Indian, who was, unfortunately, already
the mother of several children.

There is no evidence to show that Madame Giraud-
Girard was unkind to or in any particular neglected
her step-children ; but it was not long before the dis-
comforts of which a second marriage is so liable to
prove the fertile source began to make themselves
disagreeably manifest. Stephen had early found a
grievance in the fact that the newcomer not only
supplanted his influence in the family, but was also
disposed to exercise control of his theretofore comparatively unrestricted liberty ; while his step-mother,

failing to understand the peculiarities of the lad's disposition, was unable to allay the distrust with which he had immediately regarded her. Stephen had always been amenable to kindly argument, being one of those natures which must be led and cannot be driven, and no especial effort having been made to win his regard, his dislike and jealousy increased from day to day, until, since he was not at the least pains to conceal his sentiments despite his father's frequent reproofs, it required but little foresight to predict that a speedy climax was inevitable.

The crisis arrived one day while the family were gathered about the dinner-table. Some action of Stephen's had called for a reproof from his step-mother, and her attempt to correct him proved to be the final increment which the lad's overburdened temper could not withstand. Restraining his feelings no longer, he burst into a torrent of passionate reproach, expressing so plainly the bitterness of his spirit that it was impossible for his father, who happened to be present, to pass the matter by without making of it a signal example. Astounded by Stephen's violence, apparently so disproportioned to the provocation, and indignant at his temerity, Pierre Girard, as soon as he was able to stem the current of his son's indignation, rebuked him in the sternest manner, commanding him to make immediate present

2

amends and submit cheerfully to family discipline in the future, or else to find a home for himself as soon as he was able elsewhere.

But the young lad, having once lost his self-control, had gone too far to turn back. He was unwilling to confess himself an offender where he firmly believed himself to be the one aggrieved, and his father's command had hardly been finished before Stephen passionately replied : " I *will* leave your house. Give me a venture on any ship that sails from Bordeaux, and I will go at once where you shall never see me again !"

Persisting in his refusal to make amends, it was evident that heroic measures were necessary, both for the lad's own sake and for that of the family, whose peace was constantly imperiled by his unmanageable presence. And while there can be no doubt that Pierre Girard felt deep compassion for his motherless lad when the heat of his indignation had subsided, yet it was still apparent something must be done to prevent such scenes of domestic insubordination. In this dilemma, serious thought was given the idea Stephen had broached himself, and the latter remaining firm in his obstinate attitude, his father found himself reluctantly forced to surrender his hope that his son might adopt a professional career, and consequently sought a business acquaintance, Captain Jean Courteau, master of the ship Pélérin, who was about to sail for Santo Domingo, one of the French colonies in the West Indies. Finding Captain Courteau willing to take charge of Stephen, a " venture " amounting to sixteen thousand livres[1] was furnished the latter by his father, who bade his son farewell, as one may well imagine, with many regrets that the young lad's waywardness had made such a course a necessity.

This was in 1764, when young Girard was but four-teen years of age, and though he was the owner of more than three thousand dollars' worth of goods on board, his youth and inexperience forbidding a post of more responsibility, he occupied that remarkably anomalous one of cabin boy, *and part owner*, which furnished afterward the theme of some of his liveliest expressions of satisfaction.[2]

Probably his father, after having reconciled himself to the idea of his son's succeeding him in maritime ventures, was not unwilling that the latter should begin at the very foot of the ladder in his new pur-suit. The knowledge he would thus gain of the sea and of the details of a foreign commerce could not but prove of the greatest service in any event ; and perhaps too he had not wholly surrendered a hope that a single voyage would cure this headstrong folly, bringing back home, repentant, an obedient lad. But if such had indeed been his hope, he was destined to

---

[1] Somewhat more than three thousand dollars.   [2] Compare Arey, p. 7.

be greatly disappointed.   Girard did, it is true, return many times to Bordeaux, where he visited his old home, " Les Chartrous," frequently, being received by his brothers and sisters most cordially, and by none with greater warmth than by his brother Jean [de Mombrun].   But the charm of the sea had fastened itself upon the old naval commander's son, and now his sole ambition was to perfect himself in navigation, which he studied daily with devotion.

His first voyage lasted ten months,[1] and resulted in such profit, both financially and as regards progress in seamanship, that instead of his ardor having cooled, he found his gains but added fuel to the hereditary passion.   Besides, was this a time to acknowledge he had been wrong, when he had shown he could maintain his independence, though so very young?   And, flushed with success, he sailed again and again, until at the end of his sixth voyage he had attained the rank of lieutenant of the vessel.

Now it was at that time the law of France that no person under twenty-five years of age could be admitted to the examination preliminary to granting a license to command, nor could this be granted except to an applicant who had already sailed two cruises in the Royal Navy.   Girard lacked both qualifications, but nevertheless, undaunted by the fact,

---

[1] Arey, p. 7.

he determined to apply for the necessary permission, and his father's influence being still, happily, powerful enough to procure a dispensation, on the 4th of October, 1773, there was given "To Stephen Girard, of Bordeaux, full authority to act as Captain, Master, and Patron of a Merchant Vessel." [1]

Thus armed, he sailed from Bordeaux for the last time, and during the sixty years of busy life that supervened he never saw again the old homestead in the Rue Ramonet aux Chartrous, nor, save only his brother Jean, did he ever hold again the hand of one of his brothers or sisters, or of that father to whom he owed his starting-point in life.

He cleared for St. Marc's, in the island of Santo Domingo, on board the ship "La Julie," Captain Mouroux commanding, and reaching there in February, 1774, sailed thence for New York, at which port, the first at which he touched on the Continent of North America,[2] he arrived in the following July. There he met with a prosperous merchant of that city named Thomas Randall,[3] whose notice had been attracted by the business tact and shrewdness Girard displayed in disposing of the articles which he brought with him to New York, and the former taking a great fancy to the young man, then in his twenty-fifth year, their acquaintance rapidly ripened to intimacy.

[1] Compare Arey, p. 8.   [2] Will., Art. XX, § 6.
[3] Later of the firm of Randall, Stewarts & Cox.

Mr. Randall was engaged in trade with New Orleans, Port au Prince, and the West Indies generally, and not having an entirely responsible master for his ship, " L' Aimable Louise," it occurred to him that perhaps this alert young Frenchman might be the very man he needed. So, as a preliminary experiment, he offered Girard the position of first officer under Captain Malahard, and this being accepted, it led to such satisfactory results that at the termination of the first voyage he sold Girard a part interest in the vessel, and the two joined in freighting and dispatching her under the latter's command for New Orleans and the West Indies.

For two years this quasi-partnership or community of affairs continued, and during its existence the war between Great Britain and her American Colonies was declared, which immediately put American shipping, and particularly that homeward bound from the West Indies, in the greatest danger. It was owing to this apparently irrelevant circumstance that Girard first conceived the idea of visiting the city of his subsequent adoption, and the following anecdote shows upon what a trivial event the unconscious choice of his future happened to turn. In May of 1776 he found himself, after many days of fog and storm at sea, fronting a large bay, in complete ignorance of his where-

abouts, and prudence plainly dictating that he should
anchor. This was accordingly done, while at the
same time the small cannon carried for emergencies
was discharged again and again for a pilot, the sound
creating not a little excitement upon the shore, as
may be very easily imagined under the circumstances.
Upon the advent of the pilot it was discovered that
the bay was that of the Delaware, and Girard further
learned that a British fleet was even then cruising
outside, so that an attempt to put to sea or to make
the port of New York, for which he was bound,
would almost inevitably result in capture. Advised
by the pilot to relinquish his intention of going
further, he objected that he had no American
money on board to pay the pilotage up the river,
which was demanded in advance; but this difficulty
being met by the kindly offer of a loan from one
Captain King, who had come aboard with the pilot to
discover who had had the temerity to discharge signal guns under the very nose of the British, Girard
accepted his courteous offer and the anchor was
weighed. He was in the habit of saying, jokingly, in
after life, alluding to this circumstance, that when he
first came to Philadelphia he was obliged to borrow
five dollars to bring him into the city; and it was well
that he did, for his ship was not yet out of sight of
the spot where she had been lying before a British

man-of-war entered the bay, so that if they had not escaped just when they did, in less than an hour Girard would have been a British prisoner.[1]

Upon arriving in Philadelphia, he decided that the risk of putting to sea again immediately was too great, and apparently having made an arrangement with Mr. Randall, by which he sold his interest in "L'Aimable Louise," he took a store on Water Street, which he stocked with the remnants of her West Indian cargo. Before he had completed the sale of these articles Admiral Howe blockaded the port, in July, 1777, and finding that he would be compelled to remain some time in that city, he wrote to his friends in Bordeaux that a great profit might be expected, on account of the high prices which prevailed consequent upon the war, should they export clarets and brandies to Philadelphia. Having confidence in his judgment, these friends forwarded him consignments in casks, which upon arrival were bottled and sold upon his friends' account, although that he did not then intend remaining ashore after it should become possible for an American ship to safely put to sea is evident from the fact that he filled the greater part of his store with blocks, cordage, and other paraphernalia of shipbuilding, contem-

[1] Compare Simpson, p. 27; Louise Stockton, *The Continent,* June 20th, 1883, p. 773.

plating the building of a ship for himself so soon
as peace should be declared.

But though these commercial transactions demanded considerable attention, they did not entirely
monopolize his time, and in the intervals of business
he found leisure to make acquaintances among his
fellow-citizens other than merely those of the men
with whom he transacted his daily affairs, and among
them was a certain Mr. Lum, residing on Water Street
above Vine.   Mr. Lum was a shipbuilder,[1] widely
known in Philadelphia as a plain and reputable man,
with whom it is highly probable that Girard first
came in contact through his above-mentioned intention to construct a vessel, this work demanding the
advice and service of a competent master builder.

Visiting Mr. Lum from time to time, Girard soon
became acquainted with his daughter Mary, a beautiful brunette of sixteen, who was endowed with charms
that easily accounted for the admiration he at once
displayed for her.   Her hair was abundant, of a rich
and glossy black, and to a fair complexion and fine
figure she joined a modesty as noticeable as her
beauty was widely celebrated.   She was unquestion-
ably far below her admirer in social station, but all co-
temporaries agree in admitting that, notwithstanding
her great personal beauty and comparatively modest

1 *Memoirs and Autobiography of Some of the Wealthy Citizens of Philadelphia.*
Phila , 1846, p. 74.

2*

position, her character was quite free from frivolity or
undue levity, and she was, further, of a disposition
that though quite reserved was yet exceedingly
amiable. It is true that she had had but few opportunities to improve her mind through reading or
study, but it is equally true that she possessed, nevertheless, a quick intelligence, and invariably evinced a
ready appreciation of knowledge in others that went
far to render her a most agreeable companion.[1]

A curious incidental testimony as to her personal
worth appears in the letters written to Girard by his
brother Jean [de Mombrun] preceding and following
the latter's acquaintance with her; for while the
earliest of these share the indifference of Girard's
offended family to the person upon whom he had fixed
his regard, those that follow Jean's meeting with her
outvie each other in making amends for the injustice he
had unintentionally done her. It would seem that
Girard, anticipating the strenuous objections made by
his relatives to a match with one so illy fitted to
advance his material interests, had neglected to notify
them of his attachment to Mary Lum, or of the
engagement of marriage which shortly followed their
acquaintanceship, so that the first intimation of the
matter that reached his family was the announcement
of the already accomplished marriage. Even this

[1] Personally vouched for to the writer by Professor William Wagner.

seems to have come to Jean in rather an indirect way,
for in 1778 he writes: "And now, my dear brother,
tell me the news with you. They say that you are
married. I hope so, and that you are sharing the
pleasures two married people are in condition to enjoy
when they are really well matched. My intention is
to do the same, and in the same country, where the
sex is so charming,"[1] after which briefly courteous
sentences his letters completely ignore the existence
of his brother's wife for a period of nearly two
years.

This significant silence is only once broken by the
request, in 1780: " Greet your wife for me, a thing I
shall be able to do myself before the end of the
year,"[2] which promise being carried into effect, either
in the winter of 1780 or the spring of 1781, the visit
resulted in a change of sentiment so marked that it
is impossible to overlook it.

For, staying at his brother's house and meeting
Mary Girard daily upon terms of the closest intimacy,
Jean's opinions underwent a change whose signifi-
cance cannot be mistaken. In a postscript to a letter
written to his brother in 1781, somewhat laboriously
translated into the unfamiliar English tongue, in
order that its subject might have the pleasure of
reading it for herself, Jean betrays a warmth of feel-

[1] Letter from Cape François, 10th September, 1778.
[2] Letter from Cape François, 6th February, 1780.

ing which testifies cordially in favor of that character and admirable conduct on the part of his brother's wife which compelled such a radical change of sentiment. Jean says : " Be so kind as to assure my dear sister-in-law of my true affection. I long for embracing her and the familly (if she has any). If God grants my vows (wishes) I shall one day live with you both, and there, wishing for your mutual happiness, enjoy the pleasure of life," [1]—a display of feeling quite unusual on the part of its writer, and one further supplemented by many messages of regard and affection in his various subsequent letters.

In 1783 he writes in English again to Mrs. Girard herself, as follows :

" DEAR SISTER :—The sole letter I received from you (March, 1780) is fallen into my hands very often since my arrival from France, where I met with more vexations that is hardly to be described. You cannot imagine what a satisfaction and pleasure I feel in reading it, and how much I desire to receive some others, till the happy moment of embracing and express you my affection with the candour of a real friend and brother."

He is continually sending her remembrances in the shape of birds, fruits, plants, tropical preserves, and such articles as housekeepers love, coupling

[1] Letter from Bordeaux, 29th December, 1781.
[2] Letter dated " Cape François, the 20th February, 1783."

these presents with the expression of his sincerest esteem. "I am awaiting the spring in order to send some oranges to my sister. Say a thousand kind things to her for me and assure her of my unalterable friendship."[1] And in 1784 he writes the jesting message, "I hope that my dear Mary'll look around for a good match,"[2] following it with, "Many compliments to your wife. I have a couple of orange trees and do not know how to send them to her."[3] "Thousands and thousands of friendly wishes to your dear wife. Say to her that if anything from here would give her pleasure, to ask me for it. I will do everything in the world to prove to her my attachment."[4] "I send for my dear sister a box of syrups and some oranges, with a pretty parroquet."[5] "I send by Derussy the jar which your lovely wife filled for me with gherkins, full of an excellent guava jelly for you people, besides two orange trees. He has promised me to take care of them. I hope he will, and embrace, as well as you, *my ever dear Mary*,"[6] the italicized phrase being in English. "I send for my sister the trunk full of coffee and two ankers of brandy as the proceeds of her venture."[7]

[1] Letter of 30th December, 1783. [2] "The Cape, 2d March, 1784."
[3] "The Cape, 24th March, 1784."
[4] "At the Mole St. Nicolas, 13th June, 1784."
[5] "The Cape, 17th July, 1784." [6] "The Cape, 26th July, 1784."
[7] "The Cape, 24th October, 1784."

"Adieu, dear friend; I wish you, as well as your dear better-half, whom I embrace also, all satisfaction in this new year, and am forever your friend and affectionate brother."[1] "If your wife, whom I salute, wishes a little parrot, I will send her one."[2] "My compliments to my ever dear Mary. I am exceedingly sorry that I could not find oranges for this time."[3]

But, despite the light cast by these passages upon the young girl whom Girard had chosen to be his wife, it cannot be denied that it was a very hazardous undertaking to link himself permanently with one who, notwithstanding her rare physical beauty and many admirable qualities, was still incontestably not the person he should prudently have chosen. The difference in their social status alone was enough to have caused him to hesitate long before taking the irrevocable step—a difference that must have been quite as apparent to him as it certainly was to many of his neighbors, for it is not to be supposed that his keen appreciation of the deficiency in his own early education made him estimate his own position so modestly as not to perceive this gap. He was perfectly conversant with the station of his father's family in France, and, indeed, seems to have been so confident of their disapproval that he hastened the preparations for the

[1] "The Cape, 11th January, 1785."   [2] "The Cape, 29th May, 1785."
[3] "The Cape, 13th February, 1786."

ceremony in order to anticipate their objections by the announcement of the accomplished fact; and this, together with the knowledge of the financial success he had already attained, with its foreshadowing of the greater share of public attention destined to follow, forms but another of the many arguments showing the unselfishness of the motives leading to that selection which has excited comment even to the present day.

One needs not to search far for the actuating impulse which compelled this Cophetua-like prostration of tangible success and present comfort at the feet of a mere hope of future happiness in the girl's affections. He was but twenty-six years old, quite unused to the companionship of young women; entirely too self-reliant to either ask for or accept counsel from strangers in matters relating to his personal concerns; far from his family or from any one sufficiently interested in him to point out the danger of his contemplated step, and fascinated by the beauty and goodness of the young girl upon whom he had fixed his regard. And while he was, notwithstanding, so far alive to the difference between them as to determine that the success or failure of his experiment should be strictly limited to the person of the young girl herself, as is evidenced by his complete ignoring of her relatives both then and thereafter, there is no room for doubt that the sole motive which actuated him in making his choice was the sincere and unreasoning affection he had conceived for her—an affection which, notwithstanding the sadness which overshadowed her later years, still happily endured unbroken in its constancy to the day of the death of its object.

They were married by the Reverend Mr. Stringer, on the 6th of June, 1777, at Saint Paul's Protestant Episcopal Church, on Third Street, below Walnut, in the city of Philadelphia,[1] and immediately commenced housekeeping at Girard's residence, on Water Street, where they remained without event of particular importance until late in the following September.

It was about this time that Girard's brother, Jean [de Mombrun], wrote him from Cape François, Santo Domingo, saying: "Our dear father in every letter he writes asks me for news of you. * * * * It seems that we are dearer to him since the death of Bellevuë. He begs me to join him in inducing you

---

[1] It has been erroneously stated by Henry Simpson, *vide The Lives of Eminent Philadelphians Now Deceased*, that the ceremony was performed by Dr. Samuel Magaw. This mistake arose from his having merely consulted the "Transcript of Records of St. Paul's Church," where the marriage does appear to be noted under those celebrated by Dr. Magaw. Had he gone to the original he would have seen the apparent error. Consult original " Records of Marriages of Saint Paul's Church, from 1759 to 1835," where this marriage is recorded under the heading, "The Undermentioned Marriages, by the Rev. Mr. Stringer." These original records were transcribed into " Records of Saint Paul's Church, from 1760 to 1835," by John Claxton, Plunk't F. Glentworth, and Joseph Wright, who were appointed by the vestry of Saint Paul's Church to certify to the accuracy of the old records and to make a transcript of them, both of which they did on March 3d, 1806.

to forsake this dangerous commerce,[1] urging us to form a partnership with the chief house at Cape François, in which he will take part interest in order to help us. Should you wish to command a vessel, he will provide one for you."[2]

It is interesting to consider what might have been the possible result had this offer arrived a little earlier, but Girard's marriage having already taken place, he declined the generous suggestion, and Lord Howe having threatened the city of Philadelphia in September of 1777, he removed with his wife to Mount Holly, New Jersey, where he occupied a one-story-and-a-half frame house on a little farm. The farm consisted of from five to six acres, which he had purchased the previous year from Isaac Hazlehurst[3] for five hundred dollars, and during more than a year he divided his time between farming this place and making trips, by way of the Rancocas River, to Philadelphia, where he kept a watchful eye upon his property in the hands of the British, and also sold the clarets his friends in Bordeaux continued to send him. In the enforced leisure of this life he became deeply interested in the tremendous struggle for liberty with which he was surrounded, and that intense admiration for a republican form of government which comes so

---

[1] By reason of the War of the Revolution.
[2] Letter of Jean [de Mombrun], " The Cape, 27th September, 1777."
[3] Simpson, p. 30.

naturally to a native of Bordeaux soon implanted in
his bosom a hearty belief in the future of the American Nation, which he displayed on many prominent
occasions during his later life.   Deliberation led him .
to determine to cast in his lot with the struggling
States, and accordingly in 1778, two years after his
arrival in Philadelphia, he took the "Oath of Allegiance to the State of Pennsylvania" prescribed by
the General Assembly, which he repeated in the following year.   The certificate received in return was
as follows: "I do hereby certify that Stephen Girard,
of the city of Philadelphia, merchant, hath voluntarily
taken the Oath of Allegiance and Fidelity as directed
by an act of the General Assembly, passed the 13th
day of June, 1777.   Witness my hand and seal the
27th day of October, A. D. 1778.   Jno. Ord. (No.
1678.)"[1]

In 1779 he returned from Mount Holly to Philadelphia, resuming his interrupted business, and building
the long contemplated vessel, a sloop, which he
named the "Water Witch."   This vessel was built by
Mr. Lum, and her planning having been the original
cause of Girard's meeting with his wife, she was
naturally regarded by him with considerable affection.
But he went even further than this, and like the great
Dr. Johnson, who would neither enter nor leave

---

[1] *Famous Americans of Recent Times*, by James Parton, Boston, 1867, p. 231.

a room unless his right foot was foremost, Girard adopted a certain superstitious belief to the effect that the " Water Witch " could never possibly cause him a loss.

To a great extent she justified his extraordinary confidence in her, but her shipwreck shortly after the happening of the great misfortune of his domestic life, a misfortune that may not inaptly be compared to the shipwreck of his personal happiness, was a coincidence certainly strange enough to have justified his regarding her at the outset as having a subtle connection with his prosperity or failure. There is no doubt that he was impressed by this accidental concurrence, for when, long afterward, he built his permanent Philadelphia residence at No. 23 North Water Street, he placed a sheet-iron model of the " Water Witch " in the rear railing of the two-story counting-house, adjoining his four-storied dwelling,[1] as a tribute to the sole superstition of which he was ever known to be guilty.

His business affairs prospered amazingly, and on February 1st, 1780, at the urgent solicitation of Joseph Baldesqui, formerly a paymaster in the Legion of Count Pulaski, he entered into a partnership to prosecute trade to Santo Domingo and the West Indies. Baldesqui promised to sail immediately for

1 Professor William Wagner.

Santo Domingo, from whence he professed to be able to obtain the major part of the consignments for the benefit of the Philadelphia house, and into this partnership Girard, already worth more than thirty thousand pounds, put ten thousand, Baldesqui subscribing twenty thousand, in ships, uncollected notes, and the like. Baldesqui sailed for Cape François in February, 1780, where he remained but a short time, utterly failing to redeem his promises, and then left for Boston, where he remained until January, 1782, in all this interval doing nothing for the benefit of the new firm, the whole burden of whose affairs fell upon the shoulders of Girard. The latter having in the meanwhile bought from Edward Stiles, with his private funds, the frame dwelling on the east side of Water Street, in which he resided, together with three fireproof stores adjoining, Baldesqui insisted, upon his return to Philadelphia, in January, 1782, that these stores should be considered partnership property. This action on Baldesqui's part, coupled with his refusal to pay the firm the usual commission for the transaction of certain of his private affairs during his absence, together with the manifestly unequal division of labor and profit between the partners, led to the dissolution of the firm in February, 1782, and the questions in dispute being referred to arbitrators, an award was made in Girard's favor. The clear and able statement and the masterly arguments advanced by Girard in his own behalf, were no doubt largely instrumental in influencing the arbitrators in arriving at this decision, the above little-known episode of his business life being almost literally extracted from a copy of the " Memorial against Joseph Baldesqui," in his own handwriting.[1]

After the dissolution Girard continued the business on his own account, and prospered so greatly that in 1784 he found it necessary to construct a second vessel,[2] which, out of compliment to his brother Jean [de Mombrun], he named the " Two Brothers." But, despite his prosperity and fancied security, the disaster hinted at above as impending over his household was soon to fall upon it, and, after eight years of happy married life, in May, 1785, his wife began to show unmistakable signs of the frightful disorder of insanity. On the 12th of that month Girard wrote the terrible news to his brother, Jean, at Cape François, and received in reply a letter couched in language of the most fervent sympathy. Jean writes: "I have safely received your letter of the 12th of May last. It is impossible to express to you what I felt at such news. I do truly pity the frightful state I imagine you to be in, above all, knowing the regard and love

---

1 *Mémoire de S^{te}. Girard, etc., Contre le Sieur Joseph Baldesqui.*

2 Compare Arey, p. 11, where it is incorrectly said to have been his first vessel.

you bear your wife," and, after saying that nothing but the pending dissolution of his own partnership, which required his constant presence, prevented him from going at once to console Girard, he adds: " But, above all, conquer your grief and show yourself by that 'worthy of being a man, for, dear friend, when one has nothing with which to reproach one's self, no blow, whatsoever it may be, should crush him. I presume that the grief which this lovely woman has always shown to me at having no children is the cause of her misfortune, to which it is necessary to be resigned as to the will of God. * * * Adieu! I exhort you to firmness and courage, without forgetting to care for your own health so far as possible. I am your affectionate brother and friend." [1]

The affliction of Mrs. Girard, however, was rather of a melancholy than violent character, and she was kept at home, the restoration of her wavering mind being sought by means of quiet coupled with medical treatment, whose beneficial effects became almost immediately apparent. Upon the receipt of his brother's letter Girard had written suggesting various methods of treatment, among them the possible advantages of a change of climate and scene, to which Jean replies: " The last of your letters

[1] Letter from the Cape, 30th June, 1785.

announces your wife's projected voyage by the brig. If you should happen to determine upon it, without regarding the trouble she may cause me, I shall not be sorry to have her here; the less so since my care, etc., may cure her, being singularly attached to her. Although, on the other hand, should the voyage not prove salutary to her it will cause me a great deal of chagrin," [1] a letter speaking volumes for the sincerity of Jean's earlier professions of regard, though he had no opportunity of putting these kindly offers to the proof, owing to the idea of the projected voyage being finally given up. During the whole of this painful period Girard watched over his wife's comfort with the most affectionate assiduity, and at last, though still subject to periods of depression, he was able to write to Jean in such manner as to call forth the reply: "Be sure to give my love to your wife. I am overjoyed that she is getting better," [2] followed two weeks later with, "I learn with joy of the restoration of your wife. Give her a thousand kisses for me, and believe me your affectionate friend and brother." [3]

Confident of her eventual re-establishment, therefore, Girard returned to business with the ardor of one

[1] Letter, Cape Franç is, 29th July, 1785.
[2] Letter, Cape François, 28th August, 1785.
[3] Letter, Cape François, 8th September, 1785.

who has successfully passed a great ordeal, and began
to consider seriously a proposition of copartnership
which Jean had first formally broached in his letter of
26th July, 1784. To this proposition Girard had at
the time returned a favorable reply, and he now accepted the terms proposed by Jean, the partnership
being accordingly entered into, commencing on the
first day of July, 1785, to continue five years. The
agreement as set forth in Jean [de Mombrun's] letter
was as follows: (1) The Santo Domingo house was
to be at Cape François; (2) the partnership was to
commence immediately upon the expiration of Jean's
partnership with M. Hourquebie, on July 1st, 1785;
(3) the whole capital of both partners was to be put
in the firm, including all furniture, lands, and houses
whatsoever, amounting, as Jean says, to about three
hundred and odd thousand pounds. The Philadelphia house was to be styled Sn. & Jn. Girard frères,
and was to transact no business and make no purchases except for the benefit of the firm. It was to
be managed by Stephen solely, unless Jean were in
Philadelphia, in which latter case it was to be managed jointly, and all the expenses of Stephen's household (except clothing) or of the office, including all
costs of voyages or trade, were to be divided between
the partners, the partnership to run for at least five
years; (4) if Jean should renew his partnership with

M. Hourquebie, it was agreed that he was to send Stephen sixty-six thousand pounds, and further that his share of the profits arising from such renewed partnership was to go into the common fund of his partnership with Stephen, which latter society was to be charged with all costs of voyages, trade, etc., on its account, and with all the household expenses of Jean, except clothing ; (5) in case the partnership of Jean with M. Hourquebie should not be renewed, the former was to maintain alone a branch house at Cape François, under the style of Jn. & Sn. Girard frères, or else send all his money and goods to the Philadelphia house, it being agreed that either he or Stephen would voyage for the firm's benefit. All rents from Stephen's real estate were to go into the firm assets, as was also the half rent of Jean's coffee plantation of Doidy, farmed on shares, which was at that time paying ten thousand pounds a year net. Jean exacted also certain powers of attorney, and everything was to be shared between the partners equally. The letter concludes : " There must be good faith, openness, and perfect accord, and in case of my death, or of yours, the partnership must end six months after the event, for I do not wish to have any business with an heir, unless, I mean, the two members of the firm agree beforehand as to the survivor." [1]

[1] Letter, " The Cape, 26th July, 1784."

Jean did not renew his partnership with M. Hourquebie, but formed a new one at Cape François under
the title of Girard, Bonnardel & Lacrampe, which
firm were the local representatives of Sn. & Jn.
Girard frères, of Philadelphia, Jean's share of the
profits arising from which doubtless came under the
same conditions as had been agreed in the case of
a renewal with M. Hourquebie.   In March of 1787
this last was dissolved, and in the following August
he sailed, to take charge of the Philadelphia house,
on board a vessel he had just purchased, and named
" Les Deux Amis."

He had previously stipulated, however, that Stephen should not at once leave the reins of their
affairs in his hands without a most competent assistant, not, as he says, " that I do not feel myself
capable of managing them, but because, not being
acquainted, a stranger may appear to me to be good
who is bad, and one who may appear bad may be
good, which uncertainty will put me in a perplexity
prejudicial to our interests."   He also wrote that he
would not occupy Stephen's house, taking charge of
his wife, who was still far from strong, but upon
learning that Stephen contemplated her remaining
in the country during his absence, Jean consented to
occupy the mansion.   Accordingly, he arrived with
his wife and family in September, 1787, with a large

cargo of claret, and in October of the same year Stephen sailed in turn for Charleston and the Mediterranean, being absent until July, 1788.

The partnership continued with great mutual profit until its expiration by limitation upon July 1st, 1790. But both brothers felt, notwithstanding, that they were not sufficiently in accord as to the management of their commercial ventures to warrant its renewal, and it was therefore decided that the partnership property should be divided. In accordance with this determination, Hugh Calhoun was called in as arbitrator and appraiser, and his task was performed to the avowed satisfaction of both parties, awarding to Jean, it is said, sixty thousand dollars, and to Stephen thirty thousand.[1]

Jean returned immediately to Cape François with his family, and to Girard's ineffable satisfaction the former quiet and contented routine of his household was re-assumed by his wife, whose country sojourn, so far as it was possible for any one to tell, had resulted in her complete and perfect restoration to health. But in believing, as he did, that his domestic happiness was at last undoubtedly assured, he was destined to an awakening even more cruel and painful in the result than the first discovery of her terrible affliction. He had begun to make arrangements for

[1] Simpson, p. 35. These amounts are probably not accurate.

the gratification of her long-felt wish to visit France immediately upon her return to their house in Water Street, and he was in the midst of the necessary preparations to accompany her, when, to his unspeakable grief, the same signs of despondency over her childless condition which preceded the first weakening of her mind once more became apparent. A consultation of eminent physicians was called, who were unanimous in the belief that the sole hope for the restoration of her sanity lay in her immediate removal to a hospital, and Girard found himself at last forced to give his reluctant consent to this measure, which was at once carried into effect. The only hospital in Philadelphia at that time which received such patients was the Pennsylvania Hospital, at Eighth and Spruce Streets, and she was accordingly admitted to that institution on the 31st of August, 1790,[1] where she remained, uncured, until her death.

She was pleasantly situated on the first floor of the main building[2] in a spacious and comfortable apartment, with parlor attached,[3] and was permitted the freedom of the large grounds of the Hospital, being also allowed to receive visitors with the fewest restrictions possible. She is remembered by one

[1] William G. Malin, ex-steward Pennsylvania Hospital. See also Philadelphia Sunday Dispatch, 16th June, 1878, by same authority.

[2] Professor William Wagner, Lecture I. Also see Philadelphia Sunday Dispatch, June 2d, 1878; article by William G. Malin, ex-steward Pennsylvania Hospital.

[3] Professor William Wagner, Lecture I.

who visited her frequently as " a dark-haired woman, always sitting in the sunlight, still bearing strong marks of the beauty for which she was celebrated in early life,"[1] although her mind was then almost wholly a blank, scarcely even recognizing the old housekeeper, who would sometimes take Girard's little nieces, Jean's daughters, to see her.[2]

It might be supposed that with this last affliction Girard had sounded a depth of domestic misfortune to which nothing could be superadded, but he was doomed to experience a still sharper pang when, on March 3d, 1791, his wife gave birth to a daughter. The child was immediately baptized, in the presence of Doctors Cutbush and Warner, with the name " Mary Girard," and was at once sent to be nursed in the country, where, notwithstanding the watchful care of Mrs. John Hatcher, it lived but a few months and was buried in the graveyard of the parish church.[3]

Then, at length, childless and worse than wifeless, the misfortunes that had so unrelentingly pursued the married life of Girard were exhausted, and he found himself once more freed from harassing care in his household, though, alas, in what a manner! In view

---

[1] Professor William Wagner's Lectures on Girard, Lecture I. Professor Wagner, while apprenticed to Girard, was usually commissioned to pay Mrs. Girard's board.

[2] Louise Stockton, *The Continent* for June 20th, 1883.

[3] William G. Malin, ex-steward Pennsylvania Hospital.

of the sincerity of his love for his wife, her absence must have been a relief largely tempered, particularly at the very outset, by the keenest sense of loneliness, and he took up his daily life again with a desperate patience that was almost pathetic. His state of mind is well expressed in a letter written in 1804, long afterward, to his friend, Duplessis, in New Orleans,[1] in which, speaking of the routine of existence into which he first fell at this epoch, he says: " As to myself, I live like a galley slave, * * * * often passing the whole night without sleeping. I am * * * * worn out with care. I do not value fortune. The love of labor is my highest ambition."

But he was too well-balanced a man to permit himself to vaguely repine, for he very well knew that the only remedy for such pain as his was to be found in constant occupation, and, therefore, he sought to keep his mind unceasingly busy during his hours of wakefulness. He plunged with ardor into the details of the construction of several ships he was building for himself, and it was with much pride that he saw launched, in 1791 and 1792, those splendid merchantmen so long the delight of Philadelphia and the envy of other East India traders. They were six in number, named, in the order of

[1] Arey, p 5. Also quoted by P..rton, p. 239.

their building, "Voltaire," "Helvetius," "Good Friends," "Montesquieu," "Rousseau," and "North America," and together with the "Superb," a seventh vessel, which he took for debt,[1] and the "Kensington," they formed the most noteworthy part of the fleet with which he built up his magnificent monument of commercial success. He had owned, in addition, at various times, the sloop "Water Witch," the brigs "Kitty," "Liberty," "Polly," and "Sally," and the schooner "Nancy;" but these were chiefly engaged in the coastwise trade, occasionally venturing to European ports, and were quite insignificant when compared with the beautiful ships launched during these two years to trade with Canton, Calcutta, and the East. These were equipped with all the latest improvements in shipbuilding, and had such superior facilities for getting up anchor and pumping by machinery that they were always more lightly manned than any others of like tonnage leaving port. Curious to relate, they were never insured, there being few, if any, marine insurance companies in those days, and Girard's confidence in the then boards of underwriters being so scant that he preferred to insure his own vessels and houses.[2]

For this fleet he planned cruises extending over

[1] Professor William Wagner, Lecture IV.
[2] Professor William Wagner, Lecture IV.

long periods of time, and embracing ports in all quarters of the known globe. For instance, a ship would sail with a cargo of cotton and grain for Bordeaux, where it would reload with fruit and wine for Saint Petersburg, and there discharge this cargo, replacing it with hemp and iron. In turn these would be sold in Amsterdam for specie, laden with which the ship would sail for Calcutta and Canton, where tea, silks, and East India goods would be bought for the return voyage to Philadelphia. During many years the system thus inaugurated was successfully carried out, bringing great wealth to its projector and much incidental benefit to his adopted city,[1] and it found hosts of imitators who availed themselves of it with more or less advantage until the commerce of America was overthrown by the War of 1812.

The year 1793 witnessed the horrible uprising of slaves in the island of Santo Domingo, and many foreign merchants narrowly escaped sharing in the general massacre by taking refuge on one of Girard's vessels, commanded by Captain Cochran, then in port at Cape François. Some of these refugees barely escaped with the clothing upon their persons, but others, more successful, saved large quantities of wearing apparel, household furniture, and silver, with which the vessel set sail for Philadelphia, where she

[1] Parton, p. 235.

arrived safely, loaded with the valuables. It has been said that Girard's fortune was largely increased by the subsequent failure of owners to claim many of these articles, but of this no reliable evidence has ever been adduced, while both Captain Cochran and Mr. Roberjot, one of the refugee merchants who succeeded in saving nothing but a valise of valuable papers, vouched personally that all articles for whom owners could be found had been returned.[1] Indeed, Girard's books show large quantities of goods in Cape François owned by him individually at the time, on which he doubtless sustained heavy loss, not a little augmented by the ruin of the majority of the merchants of the island, a number of whom were very heavily in his debt.

Girard was now forty-three years old, but notwithstanding that during the seven years of his residence in Philadelphia he had identified himself with the largest commercial interests of that city, the opening of the year 1793 found him personally but little more known or understood by his neighbors than had he been the veriest stranger. The Saxon heirloom of distrust for all persons of foreign birth was still dominant in the recently separated English colonies, and, notwithstanding the close alliance of the newly formed States with the French nation, the

---

[1] To Professor William Wagner, Lecture I.

proverbial provincialism of Philadelphians led them
to regard their French fellow-citizen with a curiosity
largely tempered by uncertainty.   It is the common
fault of a narrow mind, whether in an individual or
in a community, to fortify its lack of information
with a vigilant suspicion, and in the absence of definite knowledge many fanciful tales as to Girard's
origin and personal habits were hazarded by such as
were willing their neighbors should believe them
better informed than themselves.   The impenetrable
reserve of their subject, who made it a point never to
deny such of these as reached his ears, together with
the personal dignity which would not suffer the
impertinence of being questioned upon private matters, no doubt lent an air of probability to some of
these stories, many of which, in the absence of denial,
were boldly asserted as facts, and grew in time to
be generally believed.   But an occasion was about to
arise which was to strip off a part of this reserve and
afford his fellow-citizens an opportunity to gain an
insight into the character of the inner man, whom
they had so long profoundly misjudged, for in the
late summer of this year the deadly malady of yellow
fever broke out within one square of Girard's residence on Water Street,[1] and gaining a foothold in
their midst, spread with such fierce rapidity that the

[1] Per Read, J., in Soohan *vs.* Philadelphia, reported in 1 Grant's Cases 505,
and also in 9 Casey 29.

consternation of the people was carried beyond all bounds. Dismay and affright were visible in almost every person's countenance. Most of those who could by any means make it convenient fled from the city. Of those who remained, many shut themselves up in their houses, being afraid to walk the streets. Some of the churches were almost deserted, and others wholly closed. The Coffee House was shut up, as was the City Library and most of the public offices. Three out of four of the daily papers were discontinued. The corpses of the most respectable citizens, even of those who had not died of the epidemic, were carried to the grave on the shafts of a "chair" [chaise], the horse driven by a negro, unattended by a friend or relation, and without any sort of ceremony. Many never walked in the footpath, but went in the middle of the street to avoid being infected in passing houses wherein people had died. Acquaintances and friends avoided each other in the streets and only signified their regard by a cold nod. The old custom of shaking hands fell into such disuse that many shrunk back with affright at even the offer of a hand.[1] The death calls echoed through the silent, grass-grown streets, and at night the watcher would hear at his neighbor's door the cry, "Bring out your dead!" And the dead were brought.

[1] *An Account of the Malignant Fever*, 1794. By Matthew Carey. Chap. IV, pp. 21, 22.

Unwept over, unprayed for, they were wrapped in the
sheet in which they died, and were hurried into a box
and thrown into a great pit, the rich and the poor
together.[1]   It is not probable that London, at the last
stage of the plague, exhibited stronger marks of
terror than were to be seen in Philadelphia from the
25th of August until late in September.   Who,
without horror, can reflect on a husband, married,
perhaps, for twenty years, deserting his wife in the
last agony ? a wife unfeelingly abandoning her husband on his deathbed ? parents forsaking their children ? children ungratefully flying from their parents
and resigning them to chance ? masters hurrying off
their servants to Bush Hill (Hospital), even on suspicion of the fever, and that at a time when, almost
like Tartarus, it was open to every visitant, but rarely
returned any?   And such was the force of habit that
those guilty of this cruelty felt no remorse themselves,
nor met with censure from their fellow-citizens.[2]

In the midst of this terrific pestilence an anonymous call appeared on the 10th of September in the
Federal Gazette, the only paper still published, stating
that all but three of the Visitors of the Poor had
either fled or succumbed to the disease,[3] and calling
upon all who were willing to help to meet on the

[1] Louise Stockton, p. 776, *The Continent*, for June 20th, 1883.
[2] *An Account of the Malignant Fever, ante.*
[3] *An Account of the Malignant Fever, ante* ch. V, pp. 28, 29.   Also, Arey,
p. 12.

12th of the month, at the City Hall,[1] for the purpose of devising some measures for the general relief. A second meeting was held two days later, and from those who attended a committee of twenty-seven, ultimately dwindling to twelve, was appointed, of whom Girard was one. This Committee met on the following day, Sunday, September 15th, and the physicians in charge laid the condition of the great Hospital at Bush Hill before them.

This was reported as being without order or regulation, far from clean, and in immediate want of a qualified superintendent and attendants, which self-devotion money could not purchase, for the entrance to that pest house was deemed a passage to the grave.[2] Upon the announcement of these facts a silence fell upon the Committee, when suddenly two men rising in their midst offered themselves, the forlorn hope of the dead and dying. On the Committee's minutes, under the date of September 15th, is found the following entry: "Stephen Girard and Peter Helm, members of the Committee, commiserating the calamitous state to which the sick may probably be reduced for want of suitable persons to superintend the Hospital, voluntarily offered their services for that benevolent employment."[3] The

---

1 Parton, p. 233.   2 Arey, p. 12.
3 *Minutes of the Proceedings of the Committee Appointed, etc., to Attend to and Alleviate the Sufferings of the Afflicted with the Yellow Fever,* 1794, p. 11.

surprise and satisfaction excited by this extraordinary effort of humanity can be better conceived than expressed. Their offers were accepted, and the same afternoon they entered on the execution of their dangerous and praiseworthy office, the management of the interior department being assumed by Girard and of the exterior by Peter Helm.[1]

" To estimate properly the value of this act of self-devotion one must call to mind that Girard was then in the zenith of his life, already a man of wealth and influence, with the prospect before him of a long career of happiness, usefulness, and riches. A foreigner and without immediate family, it could not be expected that any strong bonds of sympathy existed between him and the people of that pestilence stricken city. Before him stood probable death in its most repulsive form; certain and heavy losses were to be entailed in the neglect of his private interests; the most loathsome and the most menial duties were to be performed in person; and the possible reward of all this was a nameless grave upon the heights of Bush Hill." [2]

His persevering and decisive character was immediately felt in everything pertaining to the Hospital. Order soon reigned where all before was confusion; cleanliness took the place of filth;

[1] *An Account of the Malignant Fever, ante,* ch. **VI**, p. 31. [2] Arey, p. 13.

attendants and medicines were at hand; supplies and accommodations were provided, and on the very next day he reported the institution as ready to afford every assistance.[1] The following interesting extract from a letter written by him at this time to his friend, Samatan, in Marseilles, describes vividly the condition of things in this unfortunate city: " The mortality is so great and the fear so general that it is no longer possible to find nurses for the sick or men to bury the dead. In fine, we are in a most deplorable situation. Those of our people who have escaped the disease have fled from their homes, almost all the houses are closed, and Philadelphians are not received into the neighboring villages without undergoing quarantine. The few who have had the courage to remain have established a Hospital at a little distance from the city for the reception of the unfortunate. I am the active director, which causes me much anxiety. I do not know when the disease will cease. I am about leaving this moment for the Hospital, where the great number of the sick, who are constantly arriving, requires my constant presence."

" For sixty days he continued to discharge his duties at the Hospital, and up to the 9th of March

---

[1] *Minutes of the Proceedings of the Committee*, etc., *ante*, pp. 12 and 14.

following, when the Committee concluded its labors and ceased to exist, his name is found upon the records as a faithful attendant at its meetings. And these noble men did not confine themselves to mere efforts to stay the disease. They raised upon their individual credit the necessary funds, until public contributions could reimburse them; they supplied the poor with money, provisions, and firewood; they furnished burial for the dead; they received under their care one hundred and ninety-two orphan children (many of them infants), whose natural protectors had perished of the fever; they cleansed and purified all infected places, and they ceased their labors only when they had taken precautions against a similar calamity in future, by procuring better sanitary regulations, and a permanent hospital for such diseases."[1]

The deadly nature of the sickness may be inferred from the fact that from the 1st of August until the 9th of November four thousand and thirty-one interments took place in Philadelphia alone, from a population of not quite twenty-five thousand who remained during the plague,[2] but, notwithstanding the danger, Girard remained six, seven, or eight hours daily in the Hospital, leaving only to visit the infected districts and assist in removing the sick from the houses in

[1] Arey, p. 14.   [2] Arey, p. 14.

which they were dying without help. He had to encourage and comfort the sick, to hand them neces-saries and medicines, to wipe the sweat from their brows, and to perform many disgusting offices of kindness which nothing could render tolerable but the exalted motives that impelled him to this heroic conduct.[1]

One well-attested scene of the kind, witnessed by a merchant who was hurrying past with camphor-saturated handkerchief pressed to his mouth, gives a vivid glimpse of Girard engaged in his heroic mission : " A carriage, rapidly driven by a black servant, broke the silence of the deserted and grass-grown street. It stepped before a frame house in ' Farmer's Row,' the very hotbed of the pestilence, and the driver, first having bound a handkerchief over his mouth, opened the door of the carriage and quickly remounted to the box. A short, thick-set man stepped from the coach and entered the house. In a minute or two the observer, who stood at a safe distance watching the proceedings, heard a shuffling noise in the entry, and soon saw the visitor emerge, supporting with extreme difficulty a tall, gaunt, yellow-visaged victim of the pestilence. His arm was around the waist of the sick man, whose yellow face rested against his own, his long, damp, tangled hair mingling with his

1 *An Account of the Malignant Fever, ante,* ch. VI, p. 35.

benefactor's, his feet dragging helple s upon the pavement. Thus, partly dragging, partly lifted, he was drawn to the carriage door, the driver averting his face from the spectacle, far from offering to assist. After a long and severe exertion the well man succeeded in getting the fever-stricken patient into the vehicle, and then entering it himself, the door was closed and the carriage drove away to the Hospital, the merchant having recognized in the man who thus risked his life for another the foreigner, Stephen Girard!"[1]

The feelings which actuated Girard and the modest estimate which he placed upon these services may be best inferred from the following extracts from the very few and brief letters which he appears to have written during the continuance of the disease: " The deplorable situation to which fright and sickness have reduced the inhabitants of our city demands succor from those who do not fear death, or who, at least, do not see any risk in the epidemic which prevails here. This will occupy me for some time, and if I have the misfortune to succumb, I will at least have the satisfaction of having performed a duty which we all owe to each other."[2] " You will receive my thanks for your high opinion respecting my occupation in the calamity which has lately afflicted my fellow-citizens.

---

[1] *The United States Gazette* of January 13th, 1832.

[2] Letter to Les Fils de P. Changeraux & Co., Baltimore, September 16th, 1793.

On that occasion I only regret that my strength and ability have not fully seconded my good will." [1]

Twice afterward, in 1797 and 1798, Philadelphia was visited by yellow fever, and on both occasions Girard again took the lead in relieving the poor and the sick by personal exertion and by gifts of money. [2] He had a singular talent for nursing the sick, although a sturdy unbeliever in medicine, and in January, 1799, [3] he wrote to a friend in France : " During all this frightful time I have constantly remained in the city, and without neglecting my public duties I have played a part which will make you smile. Would you believe it, my friend, that I have visited as many as fifteen sick people in one day ? And what will surprise you still more, I have lost only one patient, an Irishman, who would drink a little. I do not flatter myself that I have cured one single person, but you will think with me that in my quality of Philadelphia physician I have been very moderate, and that not one of my confreres has killed fewer than myself." [4]

And so the brave man, who, though but a new-comer among the Philadelphians, yet stood to the

[1] Letter to John Ferris, New York, November 4th, 1793.
[2] Parton, p. 235. See *A Short History of the Yellow Fever in July,* 1797, pp. 28 and 33
[3] Arey, p. 2.
[4] Letter to Deveze, one of the physicians of the Bush Hill Hospital, appointed at the suggestion of Girard in 1793.

post of public danger when those bound to remain
by closest ties of blood and duty were fleeing, un-
censured by their fellows, having finished the task no
other dared confront, quietly withdrew to his own
house, and the panic-stricken multitudes, recovering
from their fear, returned to their deserted homes.
And what was the reward that such services merited
and obtained from the citizens of Philadelphia? " At
a meeting of the Northern Liberties and District of
Southwark, assembled on Saturday, the 22d day
of March, 1794, presided over by Thomas McKean, a
signer of the Declaration of Independence, and then
Chief Justice and afterward Governor of the State,
'their most cordial, grateful, and fraternal thanks'
were presented to those fellow-citizens named in
the proceedings, 'for their benevolent and patriotic
exertions in relieving the miseries of suffering humanity on the late occasion.' One of the citizens thus
gratefully remembered was Stephen Girard, 'under
whose meritorious exertions and peculiar care at the
Bush Hill Hospital, in conjunction with Peter Helm,
every possible comfort was provided for the sick, and
decent burial for those whom their efforts could not
preserve from the ravages of the prevailing dis-
temper.' " [1]

But this resolution of thanks, once passed, neatly

[1] Per Read, J., in Soohan *vs.* Philadelphia. Reported in 1 Grant's Cases 505, and in 9 Casey 20. See Testimonial at Girard College.

framed, and delivered, the city of Philadelphia considered its duty in the premises wholly done. No
friendly feeling toward the man, freshly returning,
pale, thin, and worn, from the house of pestilence and
death, prompted her citizens to publicly speak a
kindly word for that self-devoted heroism that had
just finished the task they dared not undertake. Nor
was there afterward found in all her limits one man
courageous enough to devote his pen to Girard's
defense when, in later years, public gossips, self-styled
biographers, joined the daily press in stigmatizing his
honorable name.

True, he was elected, in 1802, by the Democratic
party to the Common Council of Philadelphia, in
which office he served so well that in 1808 he was
returned with more votes than any other man on the
ticket; and this unprofitable token of favor was
several times renewed, being followed in 1819 by
election to the Select Branch. For over twenty-one
years, too, he served the city as Port Warden, an
office to which he was regularly re-elected. But it
remains, nevertheless, a perpetual reproach to the
city of Philadelphia that during Girard's whole life his
inestimable services, amid the reign of this terrible
plague, were almost as utterly ignored as though such
services were an every-day occurrence ; while his
fellow-citizens seemed to take an especial delight in

fastening upon him such tales as tend to show him in
the least attractive, if not in the most ridiculous possible, light—all for the diversion of that public whose
families he had rescued from most terrible sufferings,
if not, indeed, in many instances, from a loathsome
death.

But, his services having been undertaken in the
cause of humanity and not for public applause, it
mattered but little to Girard that his work remained
unappreciated in any tangible manner, and, his task
of nursing done, he renewed his attention to his business and to public matters, one of his first noteworthy
undertakings being in connection with a meeting of
protest against the aggressions of British cruisers.
This meeting was held March 13th, 1794, at
McShane's Harp and Crown Tavern, Third Street
below Arch, and, Girard being in the chair, it was
resolved that owners of American vessels had a right
to reimbursement of losses from vexation or spolia-
tion by these cruisers, and that additional imposts
should be placed on goods from States so offending.
"On the 18th a more general meeting was held in the
State House yard, at which the meeting pledged itself
'cheerfully to support with their lives and fortunes
the most expeditious and the most effectual measures
(which appear to have been too long postponed) to
procure reparation for the past, to enforce safety for

the future, to foster and protect the commercial interests, and to render respectable and respected among the nations of the world the justice, dignity, and power of the American Republic.' Resolutions were also adopted 'to extend to France and her citizens every favor which friendship can dictate and justice can allow;' to impose duties and prohibitions on British ships and manufactures until reparation could be obtained; and a committee was appointed to collect a fund for the relief of the crews of Philadelphia ships captured by the Algerine or other pirates. The fund, when collected, was put in the hands of thirteen trustees, of whom Girard was one,"[1] these trustees discharging their office with a fidelity and attention that demanded considerable sacrifice of private interests and doing infinite service to many of our unfortunate seamen who had been captured and held for ransom by those vindictive and merciless scourges of commerce.

A second public task was entered upon on the 9th of February, 1799, when he was appointed one of the commissioners to receive subscriptions for the City Water Works, to be erected at Broad and Market Streets;[2] after which, with the exception of giving a barrel of gunpowder toward the artillery salutes at the Tammany Wigwam Democratic celebrations on

[1] Scharf and Westcott's *History of Philadelphia*, 1609-1884, Vol. I, p. 476.
[2] Scharf and Westcott's *History of Philadelphia*, *ante*, p. 500.

November 15th, 1806,[1] he devoted himself for a considerable time entirely to his private affairs. The latter had by this time spread over almost the whole of the inhabited globe. Russia, India, China, and America were the boundaries of his ventures, and, with war spreading its rumors over the Continent of Europe, and the means of communication with outlying debtors daily becoming more uncertain and difficult, there was danger enough apparent in such widely scattered interests to have paralyzed the efforts of an ordinary man.

But Girard was not an ordinary man. Foreseeing plainly the complications which were about to arise, he commenced in 1807[2] the endeavor to collect his funds at some one central point, and after the most strenuous exertions, necessitating the sending abroad of special agents[3] for the purpose, he succeeded, in the course of the next four years, in concentrating in the hands of his correspondents, the Messrs. Baring Bros. & Co., of London, the enormous sum of one hundred and ninety-four thousand four hundred and ninety-five pounds thirteen shillings and ninepence.

For this he had no doubt more than one reason.

[1] *History of Philadelphia, supra,* p. 527.

[2] *Explanatory Statement to Accompany a Memorial to Congress,* etc., 9th March 1812.

[3] Messrs. Charles N. Bancker and Joseph Curwen. See *Explanatory Statement,* etc., *supra.*

[4] See *Explanatory Statement,* etc., *supra.*

First, his funds would be much more secure, lodged at any one point not on the Continent, than distributed in the hands of many bankers whose solvency, by reason of political disturbances, was a matter of daily uncertainty; and second, the commerce of the American States with European countries in general was so small that it would have been difficult to purchase bills of exchange upon them for such large amounts upon the Continent, while the credits could be easily transferred to England, whence was the bulk of American trade, and where bills upon American credits were obtainable for the largest sums without any material delay.

Perhaps it is also possible that Girard had even then before his mind the profits of the investment he was eventually compelled to make in order to secure the transfer of these funds to America when they were collected, although it is not likely he was able to foresee that deterioration of the English currency which followed the Continental troubles, and which was the first cause of his London correspondent's failure to remit. However this may have been, it was not long after these funds had been gathered in the hands of Messrs. Baring Bros. & Co., that he found they were either unable or unwilling to transfer them to America, according to his positive directions on the subject.

4

Alarmed by the suggestions of war between the two countries, and the certainty of the confiscation of his credits by the British Government in that untoward event, Girard resolved to exhaust these credits by the purchase in London of American six per cent. stocks and shares of the Bank of the United States. Accordingly, in 1810, he forwarded instructions to Messrs. Baring Bros. & Co. to make these purchases, charging them to his account, the value of the bank shares being then much depreciated by reason of the state of affairs, as well as through the apprehension of the non-renewal of its charter. After much delay in London, this was finally accomplished in the following year, four hundred and twenty dollars per share, on a par value of five hundred dollars, being paid for the bank stock, and, after additional delay, caused by his correspondents' neglect to deliver the stock when requested, after they had purchased it, Girard sent a special agent to England[1] to whom it was finally transferred, and by him forwarded to America.

The extent of this great operation having become noised abroad, Girard's wealth was brought prominently before the public, which resulted, in 1811, in an attempt on the part of James Sylvanus M'Clean and William L. Graham to kidnap and extort money from him through checks which they hoped to com-

---

[1] Mr. Joseph Curwen.

pel him to draw after they had obtained possession of his person. These men had rented a small house in Philadelphia, to which it was purposed to entice him upon a proposition to buy goods, their idea being to remove him subsequently to a small ship in the Delaware, where he was to be confined until their demands were satisfactorily complied with. The plot was discovered by Girard, however, before an attempt had been made to put it into execution, and the men, being arrested, were bound over to answer. After remaining in prison several months, the elder and instigator was declared insane, and a guilty knowledge not having been conclusively brought home to the younger, he was acquitted in March, 1812.[1]

It is to be supposed that, having acted as one of a committee which, in 1809, had drafted the memorial to Congress in favor of the re-charter of the Bank of the United States, Girard was especially justified in believing, with the majority of business men, that the charter would be renewed upon its expiration. He was doubtless, therefore, much surprised at the folly displayed in the refusal of Congress to heed the great public demand for its resuscitation; but in the interval which had elapsed between the purchase of its shares in England and the actual extinction of the bank, his

[1] See *A Report of the Trial of James Sylvanus M'Clean, alias J. Melville, and William L. Graham, for a Conspiracy to Extort Money from Stephen Girard, Esq.*, Philadelphia, 1812.

prudence had matured a plan by which he could secure himself from loss in any event. This was simply the purchase of the whole outfit, bank building, cashier's house, paper, and general paraphernalia, which, after the pending dissolution had become a certainty in the spring of 1812, was accomplished by him for the sum of one hundred and twenty thousand dollars, and on the twelfth day of May, of the same year, he reopened the old bank building under the new title of " The Bank of Stephen Girard," with a capital of one million two hundred thousand dollars, increased, on the first of January, 1813, to one million three hundred thousand dollars.

The opening of the new Bank was not delayed by waiting for the engraving of new notes, nor, indeed, by any preparatory measure whatsoever,[1] for while the new notes were being engraved and printed for him, payments were made in those of the State banks, these notes being afterward exchanged for his own. The latter bore the device of an American eagle and a ship under full sail, and were signed by himself and countersigned by his cashier.[2]   From the very outset they passed quite as current as those of the old Bank of the United States, their redemption in specie being never refused,[3] and an added stability was lent their character through the deposit in the new Bank's

---

[1] Simpson, p. 100.   [2] Simpson, pp 99 and 101.
[3] See *The National Gazette*, Philadelphia, December 27th, 1831.

vaults of about five millions of dollars in specie be-
longing to the old Bank of the United States.[1]

It was the rule of the Bank to first discount the
notes of small merchants and traders and of poor
mechanics, the balance being then applied to the
larger notes of more opulent men,[2] a preference, however, being always given to the needs of the Government of the United States. During the whole of the
War of 1812 Girard's Bank was the very right
hand of the national credit, for when other banks
were contracting it was Girard who stayed the panic
by a timely and liberal expansion,[3] and frequent were
the calls made upon him by the Government for tem-
porary loans, which calls were invariably responded
to immediately.

It was during the continuance of that struggle that
he first found an opportunity to use his knowledge of
the Rancocas River, gained during his residence at
Mount Holly, New Jersey, for, having three vessels
lying comparatively unprotected at his wharf in the
Delaware, he sent them up the Rancocas, mooring
them " stem and stern " across the stream and arming
them with men and cannon, where they lay without
molestation until the alarm was over.[4] Doubtless,
in this remembering of minute details and readiness
·to avail himself of them in emergency, lay one of the

---

[1] Simpson, p. 98.　　　[2] Professor William Wagner, Lecture V.
[3] Parton, p. 238.　　　[4] Professor William Wagner, Lecture I.

chief secrets of Girard's success, and his genius was
as strongly shown in the celerity with which he
recovered from occasional heavy reverses as in his
usual phenomenal good fortune.   In one of his letters
he says : ' We are all the subjects of what you call
' reverses of fortune.'   The great secret is to make
good use of fortune, and when reverses come receive
them with *sang froid*, and by redoubled activity and
economy endeavor to repair them."   A striking
instance of the practice of this creed is found in
his remedy for the catastrophe to his vessel, the
" Montesquieu," [1] which fine ship, after having passed
through thousands of miles of ocean without meeting
a single British cruiser, or speaking any other vessel
that could tell her of the war then going on between
Great Britain and the United States, arrived on the
night of the 26th of March, 1813, within the Capes of
Delaware, the very spot where he had so narrowly
escaped with " L' Aimable Louise " in 1776.   Precisely as had happened upon the former occasion, she
commenced to discharge guns for a pilot, thus forming a coincidence of peril in the commencement of
our two great wars with the mother country which
was, to say the least, of a very remarkable character.
The firing soon attracted the attention of a small
British schooner called " La Paz," indignantly de-

[1] Arey, p. 18.

scribed by Girard as about the size of a wood-shallop, which was then lying inside the cape, off Lewistown, and proved to be a tender to the British man-of-war, " Poictiers," of the British blockading squadron.   As soon as the light and the tide served in the morning, this small and ill-manned craft sailed up to the unresisting though well-armed " Montesquieu " and captured her and her valuable cargo entire.

The " Montesquieu" had sailed from Philadelphia on December 17th, 1810, for Valparaiso, and from thence to Canton, where she arrived on February 19th, 1812, and whence she had sailed for Philadelphia in November of the same year, having on board a most valuable Chinese cargo, the fruits of a cruise of more than two whole years' duration.[1]   The loss at his very door, after passing safely through all the perils of the sea, of this fine vessel, valued at from fifteen to twenty thousand dollars, and of her cargo, invoiced at one hundred and sixty-four thousand seven hundred and forty-four dollars,[2] neither of which was insured, was a severe trial to Girard.   But he immediately set about repairing the disaster, and after the necessary negotiations with Sir John Beresford, who then commanded the British squadron in our waters, a flag of truce was granted him by the Gov-

[1] Arey, p. 18.
[2] Statement of Case in Girard *vs.* Ware *et al.*, 1 Peters C. C. Rep. 142.

ernment to carry down the ransom money, which amounted to one hundred and eighty thousand dollars.[1] This was paid in coin, happily provided by his "little institution," as he called his Bank,[2] and the "Montesquieu," being released, proceeded up to the city, where his calculations and foresight were fully justified in the result. His books show that, notwithstanding the heavy loss of the ransom, the cargo brought such enormous profits in consequence of the scarcity caused by the war, the sales amounting to four hundred and eighty-eight thousand six hundred and fifty-five dollars,[3] that his private fortune was increased thereby in a manner that was very material.[4]

On another occasion during this struggle he displayed his readiness in emergency, for at about the same period of general panic he had a large amount of silver in the vaults of his Bank and a heavy stock of silks and nankeens in his warehouses, which seemed to be in great danger of capture by the British. Troops gathering on all sides and fortifications being erected warned him that he must take immediate action to secure the safety of these valuables, and accordingly he determined to send them to Reading. Engaging ten six-horse teams with canvas-covered wagons, he loaded three

[1] Girard *vs.* Ware *et al., supra.*   [2] Simpson, p 107.
[3] Girard *vs.* Ware *et al , supra.*   [4] Arey, p. 19.

with the silver and the remaining seven with the silks and nankeens, and dispatched the whole convoy to that town under the charge of William Wagner, an eighteen-year-old apprentice. Many amusing incidents occurred during the transit, which occupied three days, but the caravan arrived safely at its destination, notwithstanding the difficulties of pouring rain and defective roads, the silver being deposited in bank and the silk in warehouses, which had been previously engaged for its reception. It is surprising to reflect that the whole responsibility of this enterprise was rested upon the shoulders of so young a man ; but the accuracy of Girard's estimate of character was abundantly proved in the result, for much of the silk having been wet by the rains *en route*, was found to be considerably damaged when the cases were opened upon arrival. Equal to the emergency, however, the young apprentice purchased a quantity of bedcord and hung the damaged pieces in the sun to dry, after which he sent them to be dyed and re-pressed, the result being that they sold at a profit of one hundred per cent., justifying the extraordinary confidence his master had shown in him from the outset.[1]

The war so completely prostrated the finances of the United States that the Government found itself, in

[1] Professor William Wagner, Lecture I.

4*

the year 1814, at the extremity of its resources, with an army and navy clamoring for supplies, a public panic-stricken by the ominous outlook, or indifferent to the Government's necessities and in some cases actually inimical to its longer existence separate from Great Britain. Appeals to patriotism were vain when it was known the Treasury had been so heavily drawn upon that practically no means remained to purchase the supplies essential to prolong the struggle, and the only possibility of relief apparent in the disastrous prospect lay in the faint hope that an additional loan might be floated upon the Government credit. It was accordingly determined to attempt this, and the amount was fixed at five millions of dollars, the bonds to bear interest at the rate of seven per cent. per annum, while as an additional allurement to capitalists a bonus of thirty per cent. was offered, so large an amount, indeed, that even under the circumstances it was considered enormous. Large, however, as it was, and strenuous as were the exertions of the financial agents of the Republic to place the bonds, the day for the closing of subscriptions arrived with but twenty thousand dollars' worth subscribed for. What was to be done? Failure of the loan meant the end of the war, and *its* failure but a preface to the destruction of the States in detail. It was a moment for a patriot.

Girard did not, however, permit the question to
be asked a second time. Determined to stake his
whole fortune on the failing arms of the country of
his choice, once again the citizen of adoption stepped
in where native Americans saw nothing but loss and
personal danger, and set his name opposite the whole
of the loan yet unsubscribed for. The effect was in-
stantaneous and electrical. "The timid became bold,
and the avaricious fancied themselves transformed
to patriots. Those who had shrunk from it as from a
gulf of ruin, now rushed forward, clamorous for a
share,"[1] and, the danger averted, they were permitted
to have it upon the original terms, although an advance of five to ten per cent. could have been obtained
without the slightest difficulty.

The sinews of war thus furnished and public confidence restored, a series of brilliant victories resulted
in a peace, to which Girard thus referred in a letter
written in 1815 to his correspondent, Morton, in
Bordeaux: "The peace which has taken place between this country and England will consolidate forever our independence and insure our tranquillity,"[2]
an opinion justified, as we know, in the result, and to
which tranquillity Girard added not a little by writing
to A. J. Dallas, then Secretary of the Treasury, as
follows: "I am of opinion that those who have any

[1] Simpson, p. 109.   [2] Arey, pp. 19 and 20.

claim for interest on public stock, etc., should patiently
wait for a more favorable moment, or at least receive
in payment Treasury notes.   Should you be under
the necessity of resorting to either of those plans,
as one of the public creditors I shall not murmur." [1]

But from these stirring scenes without Girard was
recalled, on the 13th of September, 1815, to the final
scene of his domestic grief by the notification that
his wife, who had lingered through a painless blank
of twenty-five years' duration, was dying, still insane.
What chords of memory this notice touched can be
easily imagined.   He had sought the legislative inter-
vention of divorce some years after his wife's admission to the Hospital on the ground of her incurable
affliction ; but the bill had failed, and now in his sixty-
fifth year he found himself free through the hand
of death, but with no child to bear his name or in-
herit the accumulations of his years of ceaseless toil.
One can only guess the sad recollections of the early
days of his married life that must have stirred in his
bosom at word that the body of her whose mind had
died so long ago at last lay dying also—the days
when, secure in the affection of the beautiful young
girl he had married, the future opened to the successful young merchant in the brightest colors; the
happy period on the little farm at Mount Holly,

[1] Arey, p. 20.

followed by the contented life of their city home; and then the doubt, resolving into a still more fearful certainty, which opened the chapter now about to close. But although, doubtless, he did not attempt to conceal from himself how hopelessly his life in a certain sense had failed, he was a man of marvellous self command, and no outward sign was seen of the thoughts that moved him inwardly; only he bowed his head, and after a moment's pause, requested to be told when all was over; then, entering his chamber, closed the door, communing with his grief and bitter thoughts alone.

" Toward the close of the day, after the sun had withdrawn his last beams from the tallest sycamore that shades the garden, Mr. Girard was sent for, and when he arrived with all his family the plain coffin of Mary Girard was carried forward to her resting-place in deepest silence." [1] " I shall never forget the last and closing scene. We all stood about the coffin when Mr. Girard, filled with emotion, stepped forward, kissed his wife's corpse, and his tears moistened her cheek." [2]

The burial was conducted in accordance with the manner of the " Friends," who have the management of the Hospital. Following a hush of a few minutes' duration, the coffin was lowered into the grave, and another silence ensued, after which Girard bent over

[1] Simpson, p. 37.   [2] Professor William Wagner, Lecture I.

and bestowed a last look upon his dead wife, then, turning from the new-made grave, said to Samuel Coates, " It is very well," and immediately returned to his home.[1]

She was buried, at Girard's request, in the lawn at the north front of the Hospital,[2] a few feet west of the grave of Charles Nicholes, a native of the island of Jersey, who died in Philadelphia 31st December, 1807, having given the Hospital five thousand dollars on condition that he should be interred there.[3] Some days after the burial had taken place Girard gave the nurses, attendants, and other assistants various small sums of money as a reward for their care of his wife while in the Hospital, and to the institution itself he gave the sum of one thousand one hundred and twenty-five pounds in Pennsylvania currency, equivalent in specie to about three thousand dollars.[4]

It was Girard's original intention to have been buried here himself, and, indeed, a lovelier spot could hardly have been found within the city, the smooth lawns, broken with occasional flower-beds, shaded by tall sycamores, and kept with Quaker-like simplicity and neatness, having an especial charm for the sensitive Frenchman. But this wish was destined never to be carried into effect, and no other permits having ever been granted for interments within the

[1] Simpson, p. 37.   [2] Simpson, p. 36.
[3] William G. Malin, ex-steward Pennsylvania Hospital.   [4] Simpson, p. 37.

grounds, these two are the only persons ever buried
in that beautiful spot. The lawns and flower-beds
still remain, shaded by the ancient trees, but the
actual site of these graves is now covered by the
Clinic building, erected in 1868, they both being
under the northernmost portion of that structure,
north of the roadway which passes through the
building. They were, of course, undisturbed in building, for the addition has no cellar,[1] but no trace of
them can now be seen, the custom of the " Friends "
forbidding a headstone to be placed at a grave, and
the simple mound of earth which alone marked the
resting-place of Mary Girard having been previously
leveled.

The year 1816 witnessed the chartering by President
Madison of the second Bank of the United States,
and Girard having been named one of the commissioners, the books were opened at his Bank in the
spring of that year for subscriptions to the stock.
But confidence in the nation's fiscal ventures was very
slow in arising, and the days rolled by bringing
so few subscribers that at last it was self-evident that
the scheme would fail. Until this time Girard had
held aloof, determined to take no part unless he found
his name essential to success, but when the closing
hour arrived, with less than half the shares subscribed

[1] William G. Malin, *supra*

for, it was evident the time for action had arrived, and he therefore placed his name opposite the unsub- scribed-for stock, amounting to three million one hundred thousand dollars. Stimulated by his confi- dence, the same immediate and gratifying effect upon the public was observed as had followed his similar action in 1814, and, yielding to the solicitations of those who had become importunate for shares, his stock was sold again at par, until at last not more than a million and a half of the whole amount for which he had originally subscribed was left standing in his name.[1] His interest in all public matters was of the keenest description, and it was but necessary to con- vince him that the general welfare was at stake to induce him not only to subscribe liberally himself, but to use every personal effort with others to insure the success of the enterprise under consideration. Thus, becoming persuaded that great advantage to the State would follow the improvement of her water-ways, he was the first to furnish efficient pecuniary aid to the Schuylkill Navigation Company, subscribing, at the very inception of the enterprise, to two thousand two hundred shares of the stock at fifty dollars per share, and subsequently, in 1823, lending the Company the sum of two hundred and sixty-five thousand eight hundred and fifty dollars for

[1] Simpson, p. 113.

the purpose of better accomplishing the laudable enterprise and to establish it upon a more secure foundation.[1]

Girard was now seventy-six years of age, and, the summit of his life being passed, that slow process of vital disintegration began which reconciles the body more easily to the shock of final transition. In 1826 Dr. Monges was called in to attend him for a violent attack of erysipelas in the head and legs, by which he was confined to the house for several weeks, and which left so great resultant debility that it was some time before his vigorous natural stamina appeared to triumph over its inroads. He finally seemed to recover, however, but he evidently felt the need of a radical change of habit, for he altered his mode of living to a vegetable diet, which he con- tinued until the period of his death.[2]

It is probable that in stimulating the march of internal improvements Girard had no idea of the extent to which the movement would be carried through extravagance of State officials and the Legislature, or he would doubtless have hesitated much before committing himself as unreservedly to its advocacy as he did. His suggestions had fallen upon ground of alarming fertility, and it was not long before those in charge of public works

---

[1] Simpson, p. 143.   [2] Simpson, p 181.

seemed to have abandoned commonest business prudence in making their expenditures. It must have been evident to all thoughtful people that such recklessness could not go on indefinitely, and but few could have been surprised when, in 1829, the State found its treasury empty, with not only no means to complete improvements already commenced, but actually none to carry on the daily affairs of government, while, as a climax, the Legislature was adjourned.

In such straits an extra legislative session was convened in order to provide for the remainder of the fiscal year, but in the interval, before it could assemble, the threatening contingency of bankruptcy made it an impossibility for the State to obtain credit for the actual daily outlay of its departments. In alarm, Governor Shultz came to Philadelphia and besought Girard to make the State a loan for the purpose of bridging the financial chasm which had opened before it, to his intense satisfaction meeting with a most cordial reception from the latter, who unhesitatingly, and with the single object of relieving the embarrassed Commonwealth, advanced one hundred thousand dollars upon the sole credit of the Executive.[1] When it is remembered that there was no law to authorize the Governor's request, and that Girard was relying for repayment wholly upon the future

[1] Compare Simpson, p. 144.

action of the Legislature, a disavowal by which
of the Governor's authority would have caused him
to lose the whole sum, it will be conceded that in so
serving the State he was displaying public spirit and
patriotism worthy of the most enthusiastic commen-
dation.

This relief of the State appropriately formed the
last public act of his life, but his attention to private
business was unrelaxed, although his eyesight grew
so dim that he could scarcely walk the streets in
safety. In 1830 he was often found groping in the
vestibule of his Bank, unable to find the door,[1] and it
was about February 12th of that year that he was
struck and thrown down by a furiously driven dear-
born wagon as he attempted to cross the street at
Second and Market, on his way home from the Bank.
The wheel passed over his head, terribly lacerating
his forehead, cheek, and right ear, and injuring his
remaining eye, but he regained his feet without assistance, and walked home unaided, where the wound
was found to be more serious than had been at first
supposed. "Drs. Physick and Clark were called
in, and probing the wound, cleansed it from a quantity
of gravel and sand. He bore the pain of dressing it
without flinching, saying, 'Go on, Doctor, I am an old
sailor; I can bear a good deal;' but inflammation

[1] Simpson, p. 181.

setting in, for a fortnight or more his brain was in a terrible excitement, which a little later developed into a condition resembling imbecility.   After some weeks he rallied, but refused pertinaciously to attend to any business, saying that he ' would not be disturbed to be the gainer of a large sum.'   Finally, he yielded to the entreaties of Mr. Wolfert, and in March signed his name to a business document, the event making quite a stir in the household.   A desk was brought to his room, there was a great mending of pens (for he never used steel or gold ones), and then a long page of paper was filled with trial signatures, ' to get his hand in,' as he said.   At last the document received the wished-for signature, Girard expressing himself as quite proud of the performance, which he wished noted down *as the first time he had signed his name since the accident.*   This was accordingly done, but after his decease it appeared that he must have labored under an error, for *his will* is dated February 16th, 1830, *a few days* after that unfortunate occurrence." [1] [2]

---

[1] Notes of Henriette Girard Clark (Vve. Lallemand).

[2] It is perhaps not inappropriate to mention in this connection that the heirs of Girard have never believed it was their relative's intention to deal less liberally with them after his death than he had unintermittingly done during his lifetime. While they admit his intention to found the College for Orphans, yet the various contests which have been made over the testamentary disposition of his estate have been actuated by the conviction that his published will but reflects an adverse ascendency, gained after his intellect had been seriously weakened, by certain individuals, who from this time forward attended him, both in and out of season, with the most unwearying and pertinacious assiduity.

On April 30th, 1830, he bought eleven tracts of coal land in Schuylkill County, Pennsylvania, containing about four thousand acres, which were sold at public auction by the trustees of the old Bank of the United States for the sum of thirty thousand dollars.[1] The tract afterward formed the subject of a lawsuit between the heirs-at-law of his estate and the city of Philadelphia, it being asserted on behalf of the heirs that as to this land Girard had died intestate, the mere color of title which he had at the date of his will not being such an estate in the land as could be devised. Girard had perfected his title subsequently to his will, but the heirs maintained that his subsequent good title would not relate back and attach to his previous mere color of title in order to make the devise hold good. The city denied these claims and defended its possession under the will and codicils. The case was tried in 1851 before a special jury in the United States Circuit Court,[2] the verdict being for the heirs, and a motion for a new trial being refused,[3] the heirs were put in possession by the United States Marshal by virtue of a writ of *habere facias possessionem* issuing upon the original judgment. Three years later, in 1854, the city brought suit in ejectment

[1] Lessees of Clark *vs.* The City of Philadelphia, U. S. Circuit Court, October sessions, 1850, Common Law Docket No. 31.   Not reported.   Same case on argument for new trial reported in 2d Wallace, Jr.'s, Circuit Court Reports, page 301.

[2] Lessees of Clark *vs.* The City, *supra.*

[3] Reported 2 Wallace, Jr.'s, Circuit Court Reports, page 301.

against the heirs, but was defeated, and the Supreme
Court of the State refusing to reverse the judgment
of the lower court,[1] the heirs were thus confirmed,
after protracted litigation, in the only material portion of Girard's immense estate of which they ever
succeeded in divesting the city of Philadelphia.[2]

At a meeting of Philadelphia merchants, held on
the 19th of July, 1831, it was decided to build a Merchants' Exchange, at the intersection of Walnut,
Dock, and Third Streets, and Girard was appointed
one of the trustees to purchase and hold the said lot
until the company was incorporated.[3]   This was the
last position of honor which his increasing feebleness
permitted him to accept, and before the matter had
been fully completed he was attacked in December of
the same year by the influenza, which was then

---

[1] Case not reported.

[2] In Girard *vs.* The Mayor, and Vidal *vs.* The Same, both reported in 4 Rawle
323, certain houses and real estate in Philadelphia were recovered by the heirs. The
various Girard suits and discussions of his will are reported as follows :

IN THE STATE COURTS.—Girard *vs.* The Mayor, Vidal *vs.* The Same, 4 Rawle
323; The City *vs.* Davis et al., 1 Wharton 490; Beck *vs.* The City, 5 Harris 104;
Soohan *vs.* The City of Philadelphia, 9 Casey 9 ; also 1 Grant 494; The City *vs*
The Heirs, etc., 9 Wright 9 ; Field *vs.* The Directors of Girard College, 4 P. F.
Smith 233 (54 Penna. State 233).

IN THE UNITED STATES COURTS.—Vidal *vs.* Girard's Executors, 2 Howard 127;
Girard *vs.* Philadelphia, 7 Wallace 1 ; Girard *vs.* Philadelphia, 2 Wallace, Jr., 301;
Madeleine H. Girard et al *vs.* Philadelphia, 13 *Legal Intelligencer* 388.

See also *Ex parte* Girard, 5 Clark 68, also reported 8 *Legal Intelligencer* 150;
Girard *vs.* Ware, 1 Peters Circuit Court Reports 142; Girard *vs.* Hutchinson, 2
Sergeant and Rawle 188 ; Girard *vs.* Hutchinson, 4 Sergeant and Rawle 81 · Girard
vs. Gettig, 2 Binney 234; Girard *vs.* Heyl, 6 Binney 253; Girard *vs.* McDermott, 5
Sergeant and Rawle 128; Girard *vs.* Stiles, 4 Yeates 1 ; Girard *vs.* Taggart, 5 Ser-
geant and Rawle 19.

[3] Compare Scharf and Westcott's *History of Philadelphia*, p. 634.

epidemic in the city. The violence of the disease completely prostrated him, and pneumonia supervening, it became at once apparent that he could not survive the attack.[1]

But, as he had never exhibited any concern about life, so now neither did he display any fear of death, which was meeting him, as he had always hoped, in the midst of active labor. So fully, indeed, was he impressed with the idea that constant employment was one of the greatest duties in life, that about a month before this he had said, " When Death comes for me he will find me busy, unless I am asleep in bed. If I thought I was going to die to-morrow I should plant a tree, nevertheless, to-day,"[2] which steady courage, staying by him to the last, forbade a tremor in face of the final moment. But, so far as the city was concerned, as soon as it became known that he was seriously ill it was everywhere agitated with the utmost anxiety and interest. "Inquiries after his health were incessant; rumors as various and as contradictory followed one another in quick succession, until the excitement of the public mind grew to a pitch equal to that which would have attended the illness of the first character of the Republic."[3] Of all this, however, the dying man remained unconscious to the last, his few remaining days being spent

[1] Arey, p. 25.   [2] *The American Daily Advertiser*, Feb. 1st, 1832.
[3] Simpson, p. 183.

in a stupor, from which he did not arouse until a short time before his death.[1] Then he left his bed and walked across the room to a chair, at once turning and going back, and, placing his weak, thin hand against his forehead, he exclaimed: "How violent is this disorder! How very extraordinary it is!" and shortly after died, without speaking again.[2]

He died in the back room of the third floor of his Water Street mansion[3] at four o'clock in the afternoon of the 26th of December, 1831, aged eighty-one years and seven months, less five days. As soon as his death became known the authorities of the city, convening, decreed him a civic funeral. The flags of public buildings and of the shipping in the river were displayed at half-mast, and many public manifestations of regret for the loss of a distinguished and useful citizen were exhibited by the people.[4] Resolutions of regret were adopted by the Select and Common Councils of the City of Philadelphia, and the following advertisement was inserted in several of the daily papers:

"The funeral of the late Mr. Stephen Girard will proceed from his late residence, North Water Street, to the burial ground of the Holy Trinity Church, N. W. corner of Spruce and Sixth Streets, at 10 o'clock on Friday forenoon, December 30th.

[1] Arey, p. 25.   [2] Professor William Wagner, and compare Simpson, p. 184.
[3] Simpson, p. 184.   [4] Arey, p. 25.

" The trustees of the Bank of Stephen Girard are requested to meet and proceed together as mourners, next after the relatives of the deceased.

" An invitation is respectfully given to the public bodies, institutions, and societies hereinafter named, to proceed to the funeral in the following order:

" The Mayor, Recorder, Aldermen, and the Select and Common Councils, with their officers.

" The Wardens of the Port of Philadelphia.

" The officers and members of the Grand Lodge of Pennsylvania, and of the subordinate Lodges.

" The officers and members of the Society for the Relief of Distressed Masters of Ships and their Widows.

" The officers of and contributors to the Pennsylvania Hospital.

" The Comptrollers, Directors, and others of the Public Schools.

" The officers and members of the Pennsylvania Institution for the Deaf and Dumb.

" The officers and members of the Orphan Asylum.

" The officers and members of the Société de Bienfaisance Française.

" The officers and members of the Fuel Savings Society.

" Other benevolent societies are respectfully invited, and requested to proceed next after the Fuel Savings Society.

" In a community in which Mr. Girard was as universally known as he was useful, it is not practicable to give special invitations to individuals, nor is it supposed that invitations will have been expected. All those who knew Mr. Girard personally or by reputation, and who revere his example and memory, are respectfully invited to attend his funeral.

".'. It is customary to protract the time fixed for funerals for an hour beyond that designated. In the present instance the procession will positively move at 11 o'clock.

" ☞ The procession will move up Water Street to Arch, up Arch Street to Sixth, down Sixth Street to the place of interment, at the corner of Spruce and Sixth Streets." [1]

This programme was exactly carried out, the same paper containing on the afternoon of that day the following paragraph:

" The funeral of the late Mr. Girard was attended at the appointed hour this forenoon. The coffin was carried in an open hearse; it was covered with black cloth, with silver trappings. The extent of the procession could not be discerned from any one point, and the number of persons in the concourse, comprising the societies and city officers alone, could not have been short of a thousand. Spectators on the sidewalks and in the streets were in countless multitudes—forming an immense assemblage of many thousands of our citizens. So large a funeral, it is believed, was never before known in this city."

Another paper of the next day contained a somewhat fuller account in the following terms:

[1] *The Philadelphia Gazette*, December 29th, 1831.

" The funeral of Mr. Stephen Girard took place yesterday morning at the hour indicated in the programme published in the papers. The hearse was preceded by the police of the city, and the whole of the city watch walked beside the mourning-carriages, with broad blue ribbons on their breasts marked, ' City Watch.' Next to the mourners on foot were the Mayor and Recorder of the City, with broad mode hat-weepers and scarfs. The Aldermen and City Councils succeeded, and then a society of which the deceased was a member. This was succeeded by the officers of the Grand Lodge of Masons of Pennsylvania and the officers and members of the subordinate lodges. The officers wore their collars and jewels, but not their aprons. These were succeeded by various societies, constituting perhaps the largest funeral procession ever seen in this city, and the streets, from the commencement to the termination of the procession, were thronged with immense numbers of all ages and both sexes. The body was conveyed in a richly decorated coffin on an open hearse." [1]

" The funeral of Mr. Girard * * * was conducted in a mode consistent with the character of the deceased —with solemnity and decorum unaccompanied by pomp. The hearse was followed by five carriages conveying the females whose attendance was thought proper. Then followed the other mourners, and after them the members of the City Corporation and the representatives of societies invited, with a large number of citizens, the whole forming a procession of

---

[1] *United States Gazette*, December 31st, 1831.

immense extent and most respectable appearance. Fifteen carriages brought up the rear.

"The streets through which the procession passed were thronged, and the conduct of those assembled was that of persons desirous not of gratifying curiosity, but of paying a last tribute of respect to a great public benefactor. Respecting the provisions of the will, the chief of which are understood to be as we stated yesterday, we hear but one opinion—that they are what might have been expected from a man of consummate sagacity intent upon doing the utmost possible good to the community in which he had lived and died."[1]

Owing to a misapprehension on the part of one of his executors in regard to Girard's wishes in relation to his burial-place, the will had to be read very soon after his death,[2] and, the public being thus early in possession of the facts, the following advertisement appeared on the day of the funeral :

"The late Stephen Girard, Esq., having by his will left very handsome bequests to the City of Philadelphia, as well as during his lifetime very extensively contributed to its beauty and improvement, it is respectfully suggested to all citizens who are not conscientiously scrupulous to close their windows *at least* from the hours of ten to twelve o'clock as a testimony of gratitude and respect to the memory of their liberal benefactor."[3]

[1] *The Daily Chronicle*, Philadelphia, December 30th, 1831.
[2] Louise Stockton, in *The Continent*, June 20th, 1883, p. 778.
[3] *The American Daily Advertiser*, December 30th, 1831.

The windows of houses in the streets leading to the church were accordingly closed during the passage of the funeral procession,[1] which finally halted at the Holy Trinity Roman Catholic Church, at the northeast corner of Sixth and Spruce Streets. There the mortal remains of Girard were placed in the vault of the Baron Henry Dominick Lallemand, General of Artillery under Napoleon Bonaparte, who had married the youngest daughter of Girard's brother Jean. Owing to the presence of the Masonic fraternity, the necessary permission to do this was only obtained from the clergy of the parish under threat of legal proceedings on the part of the executors, the priests refusing to officiate, and leaving the churchyard when that Society entered ; so that after the manner of the " Friends," and amid a silence broken only by the murmur of the crowd of citizens, Girard at last was laid at rest in the heart of the city he so deeply loved.

Many manifestations of regret and encomiums upon the character of the dead philanthropist were published in the city newspapers during the month following his interment, among them the subjoined, from which have been eliminated some apparent errors of fact :

" He was always generous to the poor in times of distress, particularly in the cold of winter. Often

---

[1] Simpson, p. 187. *The American Daily Advertiser*, December 30th, 1831.

have his stores of wood accumulated in his Market Street Square been freely distributed to the friendless and shivering. His purse, too, has been generally found ready to open for any case of real distress which was communicated properly to him. * * * His unimpeached integrity, active habits of business, and promptness had given the public great confidence in him. * * * * So unlimited has been public confidence in him, that the most wealthy French emigrants have uniformly deposited their funds in his hands. The present King of France is supposed to have consigned him immense sums to be out of harm's way, and Joseph Bonaparte's specie was all safely placed in the Third Street vaults."[1]

Another journal, speaking of the personal esteem in which Girard was held by the respectable citizens of his day, adds :

" But to those who knew him in distant towns and cities as a rich banker, and only by report his benevolent exertions in the cause of suffering humanity— his uniform probity and uprightness are not perhaps so familiar. Here, however, where the field of his benevolent labor is spread open to all observers, his character for real improvement and judicious philanthropy can be well attested."[2]

At risk of fatiguing the reader, the following resolutions are subjoined, which were offered by William J. Duane in Select Council on the 28th of December,

1 *The Saturday Bulletin*, Philadelphia, December 31st, 1831.
2 *The Philadelphia Gazette*, December 27th, 1831.

1831, they having been unanimously adopted in that body, and subsequently in the Common Council :

" The members of the Select and Common Councils of the city of Philadelphia learn with deep sorrow that their esteemed and venerable fellow-citizen, Stephen Girard, has departed forever from the scene of his long and memorable usefulness. Contemplating * * * * the ultimate variety and extent of his wealth and works, the mind is filled with admiration for the man, and profoundly impressed with the value of his example. Numerous and solid as the edifices are which he constructed in the city and precincts of Philadelphia, they will constitute but a transitory record of what he was when compared with the moral influence that must arise from a knowledge of the merits and means by which he acquired his immense estate. Those merits and means were probity of the strictest kind, diligence unsurpassed, perseverence in all pursuits, and a frugality as remote from parsimony as from extravagance. The goodness of his heart was not manifested by ostentatious subscriptions or loud professions, but when pestilence stalked abroad Stephen Girard risked his life to preserve from its ravages the most humble of his fellow-creatures; and whenever sorrow, unaccompanied by immorality, approached his door it was thrown wide open. His person, his habits, and his home evinced the love of what was simple and his disregard of ostentation. Above all men most able to revel in luxury or to roll in a splendid equipage, he fared at all times alike, and within a few days of his death rode in the style of a plain farmer, rather than that of a rich banker, He was a devoted friend to those principles of civil and religious liberty which form the basis of the political fabric of his adopted country, and when in the course of the last war the credit of that country was impaired, he mainly contributed to arrest the threatened consequences. To say all this is but to aver what all those of mature age in this city must know or have heard.

"*Resolved*, That the Clerks of Councils be, and they are hereby instructed, to cause the respective halls to be hung with mourning as a mark of respect to Stephen Girard, Esq." [1]

For twenty years the body of Girard reposed undisturbed where it had been laid in the church-yard of the Holy Trinity Church, when, the Girard College · having been completed, it was re-solved that the remains of the donor should be transferred to the marble sarcophagus provided in its vestibule. "Some of the heirs * * * * objected to this transfer, alleging that the body of their relative had been deposited in the vault of the Holy Trinity Roman Catholic Church, Sixth and Spruce Streets, in accordance with his own wishes, and that there was no authority, either in the Masonic Order or in the city of Philadelphia, to remove them. It was an important fact that they had

[1] *The American Daily Advertiser,* December 30th, 1831.

been removed before application had been made for an injunction. The point was strongly debated on both sides. Judge Edward King, of the Common Pleas, before whom the motion for an injunction was discussed, took the view that the body having been removed, an injunction against removing it could not be consistently granted. The public ceremonies had also been arranged for, and finally he continued the case without making any decision, stating that if an injunction could be legally ordered after the remains had been actually removed from the churchyard, it could be as well disposed of afterward upon full argument on bill and answer and final decree. Nothing was ever done afterward in relation to the matter. * * * * Under the particular state of the case, the old adage that possession is nine points of the law became available.[1]

"The ceremonies of this second funeral, which took place on September 30th, 1851, were entirely Masonic, under the direction of the Grand Lodge of Pennsylvania, which upon this occasion permitted the first parade of the brotherhood for many years. Care was taken to present the members of the Order under the most favorable circumstances. They were uniformly attired in full-dress suits of black and wore white kid gloves (the white sheep-

[1] *Ex-parte* Girard, 5 Clark 68; also reported 8 *Legal Intelligencer* 150.

skin apron of the Master Mason trimmed with
broad edging of blue ribbon) and blue sashes
ornamented with silver fringe. Fifteen hundred
and nineteen members of the Order paraded, and
the procession, in the fine appearance of the members, the personal respectability of all of them, and
the decorum exhibited, had never been equalled
in impressive character. The procession marched
from the Masonic Hall, Third Street above Spruce, by
the most direct route, *via* Ridge Avenue, to Girard
College. Here the orphans under tuition in the institution, three hundred in number, were placed upon
the steps of the College building. The remains of
the founder were brought forth and borne by twelve
Past Masters to a platform erected on the east side of
the main building for the purpose. The Grand
Lodge was placed upon this elevation, the brethren
being arranged in close columns before it. A dirge,
composed for the occasion, was played by a band of
musicians. * * * * A Past Master then delivered an appropriate and eloquent oration and the
Most Worthy Grand Master made a short address.
The dirge was again performed. The remains of
Girard were again removed to the vestibule of the
College and deposited in the sarcophagus. The
line of Masons filed along in front of the latter, and
each brother deposited his palm branch upon the

coffin as he passed. After this the march was re-
sumed to Masonic Hall, where the members were
dismissed."[1]

[1] Scharf and Westcott's *History of Philadelphia*, 1609-1884, Vol. I (Philadelphia, 1884), pp. 699 and 700.

PART II.

SOME idea of the little-understood personal character of this remarkable man may be gained by considering, first, his appearance and the habits of his private life; and second, his peculiar methods of transacting business, these last being illustrated by authentic anecdotes, or related by surviving associates. "The time will come when he will be better understood, and even while he remains the typical man of business—allowing nothing to move him from his purposes, inflexible, impetuous, never taking back his word for good or ill, daring yet cautious, having a brain that governed his heart—he will also have credit for his sterling manly virtues. He was one of the men to whom much was committed, and when his time came to give it up, he gave it, not as money to make money, but to the 'little ones' with widowed mothers, and for the benefit of the city of his adoption." [1]

The first of these personal indices is but defectively supplied by the statue in front of the sarcophagus in Girard College, for while this work doubtless affords an excellent idea of his features at the time of his

[1] Louise Stockton, in *The Continent*, June 20th, 1883, p. 779.

decease, after they had been changed by acute suffering, it is of greatly inferior merit as regards the remainder of the figure. The face was copied from a death mask taken at the direction of Dr. John Y. Clark,[1] the second husband of Girard's youngest niece, Henriette, the Baroness Lallemand, and therefore, considering the peculiar situation of the statue, is perhaps suitable as representing the philanthropist in contemplation of the charity which closed his life, although it may certainly be criticised as but defectively presenting the great merchant whose efforts made such charity possible. The artist, Gevelot, of Paris, never saw his subject; and having been obliged to formulate the figure from descriptions by untrained observers, aided by the clothing found among the deceased's effects, the result gives perhaps less room for surprise at his failure to depict the grave dignity of Girard's appearance, than for astonishment at his having satisfied the original body of Trustees.[2] Its cost is said to have been thirty thousand dollars, but from the outset it has been compared very disadvantageously with the painting by Otis,[3] a contemporaneous criticism of which latter is as follows :

[1] Professor William Wagner, Lecture II.

[2] Compare *Memoirs and Autobiography of Some of the Wealthy Citizens of Philadelphia*, Philadelphia, 1846, p. 77.

[3] See Frontispiece. This portrait is in the possession of the descendants of Girard's brother, Jean Girard (de Mombrun).

" We called yesterday to look at the portrait of Mr. Girard, now nearly painted by Mr. Otis, from a cast taken after death. Mr. Otis has, in nearly fifty cases, been remarkably fortunate in preserving upon canvas the exact features of persons who had not in their lifetime sate for a portrait, and in the present case we think he has been even more than usually successful. There are few of our citizens who do not remember the looks of Mr. Girard, and all who saw him alive will bear testimony to the faithfulness of the portrait. This is the only likeness ever taken of Mr. Girard, as he never sate to a painter during his life." [1]

In person Girard was heavily built, broad and square-shouldered, of middle stature, with strongly marked, rather handsome features, and gray eyes, of which the right, as has been said, was blind. His forehead rose in a regular curve to the crown of his head, and his hair, worn *en queue*, was powdered, until advancing age rendered that addition unnecessary.[2] His person was scrupulously neat, and every morning his French barber, one Dorphin, came to his house to shave him, dress and powder his hair, re-tie his queue, and brush his clothes, during which operations Girard would converse with him, often giving him such excellent business advice that Dorphin eventually returned to France with profits of from

---

[1] The *United States Gazette*, December 31st, 1831.
[2] Professor William Wagner, Lecture V.

seventy to eighty thousand dollars, the result of
the adventures recommended.[1] He kept a colored
body-servant, too, one Samuel Arthur, afterward a
witness to his will; and in matters of dress he was
as particular as his favorite people, the Quakers,
whom, indeed, he much resembled. Like theirs, his
clothing, while not in the prevailing fashion, was
made of the best broadcloth, after his own directions, plain, large, and comfortable, and never
changing the cut, his coats being made by a French
tailor, in the style then called "shad-belly," a spe-
cies of dress-coat with square-cut, rolling collar,
above which he wore square white linen cravats,
which his nieces hemmed for him by the dozen.
He specially imported from China silk underwear for
his own use, and his trousers, which were very full
and large and of the same material as his coat and
waistcoat, surmounted low-topped walking-boots, of
which he kept a pair for every day in the week.[2]

Personally he was grave, but not at all morose.
Fear was utterly unknown to him, and under threats
or abuse he was inflexible.[3] He was not easily
aroused, but when angered was very passionate,
though in later years his temper was completely under

[1] Professor William Wagner, Lecture II.
[2] Profes-or William Wagner, Lecture V. Louise Stockton, in *The Continent*, June 20th, 1883.
[3] Professor William Wagner, Lecture II.

his control; and a salient feature of his character was his great love for children, for strong horses, good dogs, and singing-birds. In his private office several canaries swung in brass cages, and these he taught to sing with a bird-organ specially imported for the purpose from France, while his love for animals was further manifested in the shape of a large watch-dog which he always kept in the yard of his city house. Each of his ships was similarly provided, and he was in the habit of saying that the faithfulness of these trusty animals not only economized the employment of men, but protected his property much more efficiently than services merely rendered for wages.

His natural kindliness, however, was most prominently shown when he was surrounded by children, and it was in these happy moments alone that his gravity of manner unbent and the strictness of his discipline was relaxed.[1] When his nephews, John Fabricius Girard and Augustus Girard, engaging boys of sixteen and eight respectively, arrived from France, he not only felt, but openly expressed, the liveliest satisfaction. Knowing, however, his proneness to undue indulgence, he was afraid to keep them long with him, lest he should contract the habit of spoiling them,[2] and they were therefore hastily dispatched to Mr. Blondin Constant's school,

[1] Compare Purton, p. 241.   [2] Simpson, p. 133.

the "Mount Airy College," where they received
the greatest care and the most liberal education the
school afforded.[1] He also acted as guardian to the
daughters of his brother, Jean, after their parents'
decease, making his house their home and showing
them the greatest kindness, although in this case the
expense of education was defrayed from the estate
which they had inherited from their father. "He
never bought a shawl or a dress for one that he did
not for the others, and he remembered their girlish
fancies. They were sent to the best schools, and
after they had married from his house he petted their
children and liked to have them about, and, indeed,
felt a right to the little people."[2] And, not content
with thus benefiting his own relatives alone, he
brought up, educated, and furnished a home in his
own dwelling for several young orphaned women of
respectable family,[3] the fact that a person was without father and mother seeming to appeal most
strongly to the natural benevolence of his character.

But although he was thus indulgently fond of
young people, he endeavored, nevertheless, to keep
them constantly and suitably engaged, for so fully
was he impressed with the idea that active employment is one of the greatest duties of life, that it

[1] Autobiographie de Jean Fabricius Girard.
[2] Louise Stockton, in *The Continent*, June 20th, 1883, p. 771.
[3] Professor William Wagner, Lecture I.

was one of his favorite maxims that no man should leave off business because he considered himself rich enough. He used to say that he attached importance only to labor, valuing his wealth no more than he did his old shoes,[1] and an amusing anecdote illustrative of this creed is told of an Irishman who had applied to him for work. This being a form of appeal that touched Girard's theories very nearly, he was quite willing to assist the applicant, but having no actual work that needed to be done, he considered it an excellent opportunity to illustrate his theory that the pleasure of labor lay in the simple gratification of finding oneself employed. Accordingly, engaging the man for a whole day, he directed the removal from one side of his yard to the other of a pile of bricks which had been stored there awaiting some building operations; and this task, which consumed several hours, being completed, he was accosted by the Irishman to know what should be done next. " Why, have you finished that already?" said Girard, " I thought it would take all day to do that. Well, just move them all back again where you took them from ; that will use up the rest of the day," and upon the astonished Irishman's flat refusal to perform such fruitless labor, he was promptly paid and discharged, Girard saying at the same time, in rather

---

[1] *The American Daily Advertiser*, February 1st, 1832.

an aggrieved manner, " I certainly understood you
to say when you came that you wanted *any* kind
of work."

Doubtless he was himself amused at the failure of
this instructive experiment, but being very tenacious
in adherence to an opinion when once deliberately
adopted, he still maintained his theory that labor was
the one thing to be highly esteemed, and gave practi-
cal illustrations of his belief in the conduct of his
daily life. He valued always the thing itself, not
the name, which may perhaps explain why, being
an ardent republican, according to the French comprehension of the term, he nevertheless associated
himself with the Democratic party in America.
He was convinced that the principles of true re-
publicanism were most firmly secured by the creed
of the latter, and accordingly allied himself with
it, although, being keenly alive to the duties of a
good citizen, he never permitted questions of party
to interfere with the respect he manifested toward
men in public office. Prominent among those whom
he highly regarded was Thomas Jefferson, and he
frequently expressed great veneration for the ex-Pres-
ident, John Adams, while he seemed to admire no less
the talents and patriotism of the son, John Quincy
Adams. His regard for both of the latter seemed to
arise chiefly from the great services their family had

rendered the country,[1] an observance of patriotic duty very close to the heart of Girard, and one which he had on many occasions had opportunity to manifest as an infinitely respected motive controlling his own actions.

His individual habits shared the regularity and method that disciplined his business life, and were only suffered to be broken in upon when press of affairs demanded his personal supervision. He rose early, breakfasting between six and eight o'clock, according to the season of the year, making a hearty "American" breakfast of coffee or tea, meats and fish, the family usually following him about an hour later. He then devoted himself to business affairs in his counting-room until ten o'clock, when his presence was demanded by the discount hours at his Bank, which lasted until eleven, after which, in summer time, he would drive to his farm in Passyunk Township.[2] He is said to have had a singular aversion to riding in a carriage,[3] and his yellow-bodied gig, made in the height of the then prevailing mode by a Mr. Clayton, one of the best builders in Philadelphia,[4] was drawn by a single large and powerful horse of full-blooded stock.[5] His preference

---

[1] Simpson, p. 141.   [2] Professor William Wagner, Lecture II.
[3] Simpson, p. 169.
[4] Professor William Wagner: "My father drove an exact counterpart, by the same maker."—Lecture II.
[5] *Lives of Eminent Philadelphians*, by Henry Simpson, p. 416.

for walking on all occasions and in every state of the weather, however, which lasted even to the latest days of his life, led him to use this vehicle seldom or never, except to ride out to his farm; and, before age had shorn him of his prodigious muscular strength, he as frequently walked to and from his plantation as he rode. He was not a little proud of his pedestrianism, and, in the hottest days of summer, often walked to the shipyard morning and evening when he was building a vessel, which being one of the most remote yards in Kensington, the feat, added to his other perambulations throughout the city, was not at all an inconsiderable one.[1]

In winter the daily visit to the farm was usually deferred until after dinner, which meal, whether he dined at home or in the country, was always taken between one and two o'clock.[2] At this great feast of the day, as at all other times, everything that could minister to the family's comfort and convenience was provided in the greatest abundance. The table was furnished with the best meats the market afforded, and with vegetables and fruits of all kinds from his farm in profusion. The house was, further, at all times kept bountifully supplied with fruits of his own raising during their season, which were always freely accessible

---

[1] Professor William Wagner, Lecture IV. Compare Simpson, p. 169.
[2] Professor William Wagner, Lecture V.

to the apprentices in the counting-house, who were, in general, not at all slow to avail themselves of such a privilege.[1] At dinner he drank the best French claret, which he imported for himself, and of which he was a competent judge, rarely touching the heavier wines, and being at all times very abstemious as to quantity. He had, further, a custom of taking a tablespoonful of Holland gin at about four o'clock in the afternoon, which he imported in stone crocks for his especial use;[2] but his favorite beverages were cider in season and coffee of a strength seldom tasted by others, which latter, however, owing to the iron strength of his constitution, never affected his nerves in the slightest.[3]

In the country he literally kept no table at all, but satisfied his appetite with bread, cheese, and claret or strong coffee, to which he added various vegetables from his farm, making this hasty luncheon while standing at a buffet. The bread and claret he always carried with him from town in his chaise box,[4] and, on returning home, supplied their place with three or four gallons of milk in a demijohn and a kettle of butter for his home use.[5] He took no supper at all, except occasionally a biscuit and a glass of water

---

[1] "Of these facts I have personal knowledge, as I have partaken of meals at his table with his family hundreds of times."—Professor William Wagner, Lecture II.
[2] Professor William Wagner, Lecture II.   [3] Simpson, note to p. 241.
[4] Simpson, note to p. 241, *supra.*   [5] Professor William Wagner, Lecture V.

previous to going to bed,[1] and upon returning from
the farm, usually about seven o'clock in the evening,
he went immediately to his office, which was open for
business until half-past seven, although, when affairs
pressed, the apprentices were often occupied until
eight or sometimes nine o'clock. Later in the evening his confidential clerk, John H. Roberjot, read
to him the letters received during the day, or else left
them opened on his desk in the private counting-
house, after consulting which, Girard gave directions
for the following day, writing rough drafts of replies,
which, if unfinished in the evening, were completed
the next morning before going to the Bank.[2] At
about twelve o'clock he nominally went to bed,
although not by any means invariably to sleep, for he
sometimes remained awake until one o'clock, or even
later, according as business claimed his vigils or the
incessant activity of his mind prevented sleep.[3]

His chief relaxation was the management of his
farm of five hundred and sixty-seven acres,[4] which,
as has been stated above, was situated in what was
formerly Passyunk Township. In the supervision of
this he took the keen interest of a man who finds in a
favorite pursuit at once the most effective means

---

[1] Simpson, p. 165.   [2] Professor William Wagner, Lecture V.
[3] Simpson, p. 165.
[4] *Vide* Philadelphia *vs.* Girard's Heirs, 9 Wright's Pennsylvania Supreme Court
Reports, p. 12.

of preserving his physical health and a relief from the multiplicity of cares overburdening a restless mind. When he found himself unable to make his daily visit, an apprentice, charged with the minutest directions for the labors of the day, was sent in his stead, for in this, as in all other matters, he left nothing to hazard or to the unguided discretion of subordinates. As soon as he stepped from his chaise the work he had planned to do was at once commenced, and he superintended in person all the farm operations, in which task he took the greatest pleasure. Few of his vessels ever sailed for distant places without taking out orders for choice plants, seeds, or fruit-trees, which new varieties of fruits and flowers were gradually extended throughout the neighborhood, much of the celebrity which the markets of Philadelphia have enjoyed being thus due to his enterprise and love of such pursuits.[1]

He had two stalls in the South Second Street Market, where the produce of his farm was sent to be sold, and this was of such remarkably excellent quality that its immediate sale at prices above the ruling rates was always assured. In addition, he reared, fattened, and killed, every December, from one hundred and fifty to two hundred oxen for the provisioning of his ships, and this period was one

[1] Compare Arey, p. 20.

of the greatest tribulation to such of the apprentices as were obliged to attend to the little-relished duty of selling the fat and hides. Every part of the animals thus killed was utilized after the most approved methods of experimental farming, and Girard demonstrated practically the great value to a farmer of economical administration, for his products, although of a most superior quality, as has been said above, were nevertheless put upon the market at so much less cost than his neighbors', that they could have been sold profitably at the same rates had not the demand justified a considerable advance.[1]

Girard also took the greatest interest in domestic architecture, and from almost the beginning of his permanent residence in Philadelphia to the time of his death, he was more or less constantly occupied in the erection of buildings. The first of these was his dwelling, No. 23 North Water Street, with the storehouse and counting-room adjoining, and a warehouse on the wharf, which were built about 1800, and which were soon followed by the splendid stores facing his dwelling and by his house upon the Dutilh estate, on Second Street below Spruce. Some time afterward he built the dwellings on Third Street, below his Bank, following them with a whole square on Brown Street, and still later, having purchased the

plot of ground bounded by Eleventh, Twelfth, Chestnut, and Market Streets, from Thomas Dunlap, for
the sum of one hundred and twelve thousand dollars,[1] he commenced the erection of dwellings covering
the entire square of land, some of which were still in
the course of construction at the time of his death.
The majority of the bricks for these last were made
from clay found on the premises,[2] and Girard used to
buy whole rafts of lumber at a time, storing it upon
this square to season until ready to be used, the
circumstance indirectly giving rise to quite a curious
event.   This was the capture of a number of thieves
who had been committing numerous daring burg-
laries in various parts of the city, a cave being acci-
dentally discovered beneath the immense piles of
lumber which had been excavated by them for
the purpose of storing the goods they had stolen, and
in which they were eventually captured, like rats in a
hole, surrounded by large quantities of various articles of plunder.[3]

Girard usually projected the style and plan of his
buildings himself, invariably refusing the dictation or
suggestions of another,[4] and they were built in the
most substantial manner, their owner taking the greatest satisfaction in solid construction.   Many sanitary

1 Professor William Wagner, Lecture V.
2 Professor William Wagner, Lecture II.
3 Professor William Wagner, Lecture V.   4 Simpson, p. 170.

precautions were for the first time introduced into Philadelphia in these houses, and the operations of the builders were inspected by Girard from day to day with the keenest attention. But his chief triumph, and the most interesting of all the dwellings he designed, was the first one erected by him in Philadelphia. This was his residence, No. 23 North Water Street, which united in a happy combination both comfort and a very considerable degree of elegance, the house being a four-story brick, whose sloping, copper-covered roof terminated in a ridge, surmounted by a railing and flanked by two great brick chimneys. The façade presented two doors, one leading to his private counting-room, which, after the European custom, was the first floor front room of his house, and the other forming the main entrance of the dwelling.[1] The vestibule of this latter was paved with white and black marbles in diamond pattern, the same being carried back to and forming the floor of a transverse hallway and of the dining-room, which last was upon the same floor immediately back of the private counting-house, the two rooms communicating by a door across the transverse hall. Back of the dining-room was the tile-paved kitchen, and a door at the junction angle of the two halls led to the public count-

---

[1] See water-co'or sketch of this house at " The Library Company of Philadelphia, Locust Street Branch," a duplicate of which is also preserved at the Girard College. See also cut of same in Scharf and Westcott's *History of Philadelphia*, p. 631.

ing-house, built upon an adjoining lot, from which in turn access could be had to a range of fire-proof stores, still further back upon the adjoining lot. The marble pavement of the dining-room, delightfully cool in summer, was covered in winter with heavy Turkey carpet, and the floor of the private counting-house, which was of hard woods and stained, was similarly provided during the continuance of cold weather. The furniture of this office was of the simplest character, its only ornament being a Chinese drawing of his ship, " Montesquieu," presented by one of his super-cargoes. Two canary birds, cared for by the ladies of the family, swung in cages, and Girard amused him-self at odd moments by teaching them to sing with an imported bird-organ that stood upon a little table. He sat and wrote at a mahogany desk, by the side of which stood a small fire-proof safe, about four and one-half feet high, with two doors and a marble top; and this last was piled high with French editions of Voltaire, Montesquieu, and Rousseau, completing the inventory of the furniture. An even greater simplicity marked the public counting-room. One single and one double pine desk, mutilated by the knives of the apprentices, rough, lettered, and notched; a good desk of walnut, used by Roberjot; three or four chairs, and the same number of maps upon the walls, constituted the whole outfit of the office, where more

business was done than in any other in the city of
Philadelphia. The windows of his house were case-
mented, and vaults in the cellar provided storage for
the wines he imported for his private use. The sanitary arrangements were especially considered, among
others a marble bath-room being provided, and this
was justly regarded a very unusual luxury, owing to
the scarcity of water, street mains being a convenience
not yet understood in the city.

Another great innovation was the introduction
of open coal fires throughout the house and in the
counting-rooms ; and Girard designed ingenious sheet-
iron shutters, sliding up and down in iron grooves let
into the front masonry of the brick hearths, completely doing away with risk of fire from sparks
thrown off into the room at night. He brought a
cargo of coal from England, which lasted him more
than a year, storing it upon his wharf, and this novel
form of fuel burning in the counting-house fire-place
attracted considerable attention, its use being then
practically unknown in Philadelphia.[1]

The drawing-rooms occupied the whole second floor,
and were furnished in what was in those days termed
elegance, though now they would be styled plainly
comfortable. The black ebony chairs were imported
from France, a present from his brother Etienne, the

[1] Professor William Wagner, Lecture V.

seats being of crimson velvet plush, which, with the dark Turkey carpet covering the floor, formed an effective contrast to various pieces of marble statuary purchased in Leghorn by his brother Jean [de Mombrun] and disposed in various parts of the room.   There was a tall writing cabinet containing a six-cylindered mechanical organ, playing a great number of airs, which had been given him by the ex-King of Spain, and in the rear parlor was a table, also brought from Leghorn, the top of which was inlaid with particolored marbles.[1]

The sleeping-apartments were upon the third floor, Girard's own bedroom being in the rear, and the general aspect of these rooms was of that plain, simple, and uncostly character that one would expect to find in the mansion of a respectable citizen having no reputation for unusual wealth.   On his bedroom table he kept, unloaded, a brace of splendid blunderbusses, of Ketland's make, of admirable workmanship, with brass barrels and steel bayonets, that appeared never to have been used.   In one corner stood a little, old-fashioned mahogany desk and bookcase, the latter containing a small collection of books, and colored prints representing the female negroes of Santo Domingo, hung upon the walls.   A small print of his Bank was so placed that his first waking glance

---

[1] Professor William Wagner, Lecture V.   These articles are now preserved at the Girard College.

must necessarily light upon it, and from his windows the range of fire-proof stores, reserved for his choice merchandise and the best parts of his India cargoes, formed the most prominent object visible. The attics were reserved for the servants' sleeping-apartments, and from the balcony upon the roof and from the front windows of the house was presented a prospect of the glistening waves of the majestic Delaware, with his great ships riding easily at anchor, or moored at the wharf, receiving their valuable lading.[1]

To this house came frequently Joseph Buonaparte, Comte de Survilliers, brother of the Emperor Napoleon I of France, and himself ex-King of Spain and of Naples, who, being at liberty to come any Sunday to dinner, availed himself of the privilege with considerable regularity. His gentlemen followers were included in this hospitable invitation,[2] and scarcely a Sunday passed without witnessing a gathering of some of the most noted Frenchmen of the day around Girard's table, among them being the Prince Murat and Baron Henry Dominick Lallemand, who, with his brother Charles, formed part of the Court at Bordentown. At these courteous festivities the convivial element was restrained by the presence of Girard's nieces, young women, aged twenty-three, twenty, and eighteen years respectively, whose affable and well-

---

[1] Simpson, pp. 163 and 164, and Professor William Wagner, Lecture V.
[2] Professor William Wagner, Lecture V.

bred deportment added not a little charm to the informality of the gatherings. Indeed, the attractiveness of the youngest, Henriette, proved irresistible to the Baron Henry Dominick Lallemand, and in the year 1817 she consented to become his wife, the ceremony being performed October 20th, 1817, at St. Augustine's Roman Catholic Church, on Crown Street above Race.[1]

"The Count," as the ex-King Joseph was usually called, having built his house in the magnificent park at Bordentown, N. J., and having constituted Girard his banker, was in the habit of coming to Philadelphia frequently, almost invariably calling at Girard's house, where, if the latter was not at home, he would sit awhile in the public counting-house, conversing very affably with the head clerk, and occasionally with the apprentices. On one occasion, one or two of the more discreet of these latter were notified to remain after the close of the usual business hours, and far on toward morning a heavy wagon, bearing several large boxes, and conducted by three or four men, drove up to the counting-house door. The boxes, which were extremely weighty, were deposited with care in the fire-proof storehouses, where they were watched by the men concerned in their arrival, until the opening of the Bank on the following day

[1] Record's of St. Augustine's Church, Vol. I, p. 33.

permitted their removal to its vaults. The contents of these boxes, which were carefully sealed with wax, was hinted at by no one, but after some days it leaked out to those in the counting-room, perhaps through the medium of Roberjot, that they were actually the receptacles of the crown jewels of the Kingdom of France. When or how they were returned there remains a mystery, but it is probable that this report was at least partially erroneous, it being more likely that if the boxes really contained such articles, they were rather the jewels of Naples or of Spain, which, having once been in the possession of Joseph Buonaparte, were most likely to have been the ones in question.

It will be remarked that upon this, as upon many other occasions, Girard reposed a *trust* in certain of his apprentices that was, to say the least, unusual; but his judgment in this respect was so accurate that he rarely had occasion to regret his confidence. He entrusted certain of them, notably William Wagner and Meredith Calhoun, with business operations of the most responsible character, and, in general, had a full quota of them on his farm, in his counting-house, and upon his ships. They were invariably the sons of gentlemen or retired merchants, and were sent on long voyages as supercargoes, thus enabling them to gain a handsome

6*

remuneration through commissions on purchases and sales of his rich Eastern cargoes.[1] All of them entered his service free of charge, this exception to the general rule of apprenticeships having been made on account of friendship for their fathers, and, beside being carefully taught and supervised, they had the advantage of seeing the world and mingling with men of business under the patronage and protection of one whose mercantile fame had spread to the four quarters of the globe. The sole conditions exacted in return were good behavior and implicit obedience of orders, the rigidity with which the former was demanded being well set out in the following extract from a letter to Captain Bowen, of his ship Voltaire, about to sail for Canton, in 1815 :

"I desire you not to permit a drunken or immoral man to remain on board of your ship. Whenever such a man makes disturbance, or is disagreeable to the rest of the crew, no matter who he is, discharge him whenever you have the opportu-

---

[1] An incomplete list of Girard's apprentices is as follows :

(*a*) Martin Bickham,	(*f*) ——— Taylor,
(*b*) Meredith Calhoun,	(*g*) Louis Vanuxem,
(*c*) John Charnock,	(*h*) William Wagner,
(*d*) John Greland,	(*i*) Samuel Wagner
(*e*) Mahlon Hutchinson,	(*j*) John Warder.

(See Professor William Wagner's Lecture I.) Martin and George Bickham settled in the Isle of Mauritius, Martin afterward becoming American Consul there and returning to America with a moderate fortune. Many of these apprentices are ancestors of well-known Philadelphians of to-day. Professor William Wagner is the sole apprentice now living (1884), the fortune he has accumulated during a long life-time being devoted to the founding of the " Wagner Free Institute of Science " in Philadelphia.

nity. And if any of my apprentices should not conduct themselves properly, I authorize you to correct
them as I would myself, my intention being that they
shall learn their business, so after they are free they
may be useful to themselves and to their country."[1]

Girard was equally inflexible in requiring a minute
obedience to the concise directions for every emergency which he invariably furnished. " Break
owners, not orders," was the maxim of his service,
and the rule was strictly enforced, as was illustrated
in the case of a young supercargo sent to the Red
Sea. This young apprentice was to have gone
first to London, then to Amsterdam, and so from port
to port, selling and buying, until at last he was
to go to Mocha, buy coffee, and immediately return
to Philadelphia.

" At London, however, the young fellow was
charged by the Barings not to go to Mocha, or
he would fall into the hands of pirates. At Amsterdam they told him the same thing. Everywhere
the caution was repeated ; but he sailed on until he
came to the last port before Mocha. Here he was
consigned to a merchant who had been an apprentice
to Girard in Philadelphia—for this happened when
Girard was an old and rich man—and he, too, told
him he must not dare venture near the Red Sea.
The supercargo was now in a dilemma. On one side

[1] Arey, p. 17.

was his master's order; on the other, two vessels, a valuable cargo, a large amount of money." The merchant knew Girard's peculiarities as well as did the supercargo, but he thought the rule of the service might for once be governed by discretion. "'You'll not only lose all you have made,' he said, 'but you'll never go home to justify yourself.' The young man reflected. After all, the object of his voyages was to get coffee, and there was no danger in going to Java, so he turned his prow, and away he sailed to the Chinese seas. He bought coffee at four dollars a sack and sold it in Amsterdam at a most enormous advance, and then went back to Philadelphia in good order, with large profits, sure of approval. Soon after he entered the counting-room Girard came in;" he looked at the young fellow, neither greeting, welcoming, nor congratulating him, but after a moment, shaking his angry hand, he simply said: " What for did you not go to Mocha, sir ?" and turned his back, utterly ignoring the explanation.[1] But no more was ever said upon the subject, for he never scolded his apprentices, his opinion of an employé being expressed by cutting down a salary, or, if matters had gone so far that this was not sufficient, by the offender's summary dismissal. He had no patience with incompetence, and neither time nor

[1] Louise Stockton, *The Continent*, June 20th, 1883, p. 774 *et seq.*

the desire to educate people generally in business habits. Each man felt he was watched, and so long as he did his best, and his best suited, he was confident of the most impartial justice. Honesty, soberness, and punctuality were exacted, and no plans were suffered to be thwarted by independence on the part of subordinates. They were enjoined at the outset to leave business in the office, so no one of them gossiped to his friends over Girard's affairs, and the secrecy of his operations was secured by the habit of entrusting a matter of business to the smallest number of persons that could properly perform it.[1]

Several anecdotes are told which illustrate his method of rebuking his employés, one of which is that of an apprentice[2] who, in making up an account, credited a tanner with three hundred dollars more than he was entitled to. Having drawn a check for that amount, he forwarded it with the account to the creditor, who, at once discovering the mistake, returned the letter and enclosures to Girard. The latter said nothing to the apprentice, but contented himself with silently laying the letter and check upon the former's desk, where it was discovered by him the morning after the occurrence, this being the only reproof the act of carelessness ever received. On another occasion, small sums of money having been

---

[1] Louise Stockton, *ante*, p. 774 *et seq.* Professor William Wagner, Lecture II.
[2] Related by Professor William Wagner of himself.

missed from the counting-house, the errand boy was suspected of the thefts, and being watched, was at last caught in the act. Instead of the severe punishment which might naturally have been expected to follow, however, Girard merely directed that a new and more intricate lock should be obtained for the money-drawer, and this being accordingly done, the matter was passed by without further comment. Girard probably felt that the remorse shown by the lad was a sufficient token of his repentance, but it was such acts of judicious forbearance toward his employés, at times when they were undoubtedly derelict, that implanted in the bosoms of the better of them such personal admiration and regard as grew in time almost to veneration.

Another incident, not exactly in line with those just narrated, hinges upon the ungoverned temper of Girard's future malevolent biographer, Stephen Simpson, and was undoubtedly a potent cause of the malice that individual so freely displayed in his miscalled *Biography of Stephen Girard.* This work, which was published in 1832,[1] immediately after Girard's death, was the first attempt to give the general public a history of the life of their benefactor, and, notwithstanding many glaring absurdities, contains sufficient truth to have naturally formed the

[1] *Biography of Stephen Girard.* By Stephen Simpson, Philadelphia, 1832. Reprint King & Baird, 607 Sansom Street, 1867.

chief authority for the majority of subsequent sketches. In view, therefore, of the willful manner in which many facts have therein been distorted, the present writer considers it justifiable to rescue from oblivion an anecdote which, while displaying one reason for the author's resentment, at the same time forcibly illustrates Girard's peculiar method of dealing with unruly subordinates.

Upon one occasion, Simpson, having assaulted, without provocation, a fellow-bookkeeper named Joseph Clay, injured him so severely about the head that his victim was unable to leave the house for more than a week. The attack having been made in the Bank during business hours, and knowing how unjustifiable his action had been, Simpson naturally feared that he would infallibly be dismissed as soon as the matter was brought to Girard's notice. His surprise was very great, therefore, to find the day pass by without any attention having apparently been given to his outrageous conduct, but when the following morning arrived, a letter from Girard was laid upon his desk, curtly announcing that thenceforth his salary was reduced from fifteen hundred to one thousand dollars per annum. "On receipt of the note Simpson's temper knew no bounds, and I do not entertain a doubt that from that moment he determined to be revenged upon Mr. Girard for having dared to so pun-

ish and humiliate him."[1] But, necessity compelling
him to accept the reduced salary, " he had to bide his
time, awaiting an opportunity, and when this was furnished in the death of his benefactor,[2] his ingenuity
(and hope that the work might be profitable) suggested the abominable method of retaliation he
adopted."[3]

It is but just to say that the work bears upon every
page evidence of its hasty and unrevised preparation,
and it is possible, therefore, that had the author not
been pressed for time he might have stricken out the
painfully prominent evidences of his malicious purpose. But this was never done, and the work remains in its original shape, a monument of its author's
ingratitude, which, one is compelled to believe, sober
second thought would never have contented him to
leave as the only memorial in the world that one of
his name ever existed.

Girard's memory for facts, places, and business
events was most remarkable. On one occasion he
greatly surprised one of his apprentices[4] by guessing
within one hundred thousand dollars, and without re-
ferring to his books, the exact state of his account
with Messrs. Baring Bros. & Co., of London. The

[1] Professor William Wagner, Lecture IV.
[2] Simpson himself admits (p. 123) that, having become a bankrupt, he was forced
to rely upon Girard for employment.
[3] Professor William Wagner, Lectures II and IV.
[4] Told by Professor William Wagner of himself.

amount then due him was two millions and a quarter, and the account covered a period of two years, during which it had fluctuated by millions,[1] but it was evident Girard had closely followed each one of the transactions, and further, that he carried in his mind at all times a very approximate estimate of the condition of his ventures. He was himself well aware of his superiority in this respect, and was consequently extraordinarily careful in making promises to be performed in the future, for he never forgot any obligation he had entered into, and what he once bound himself to do he never after sought a pretext to evade or violate.[2] He seemed but imperfectly to realize the inferiority of memory of many of his neighbors, for he often lent large sums of money to his business acquaintances without interest or note, and upon the mere exchange of checks, on one occasion, in the case of a Frenchman named Montmollin, the loan having amounted to ten thousand dollars.[3] Nor was his mental activity confined solely to business affairs. He read with close attention the works of the Voltairean school of philosophers, and his native wit, sharpened by this active course of training, often stood him in excellent stead. It is related that the banker, Ridgway, the father of Madame Rush, having once lost his temper with Girard, exclaimed, pettishly,

[1] Professor William Wagner, Lecture II.
[2] Simpson, p. 139.   [3] Professor William Wagner, Lecture II.

" Friend Girard, thee assumes too much pride in thy dealings ; I can both buy thee and sell thee," but was quite unprepared for the retort that flashed instantly from the lips of his ready antagonist : " And I, Friend Ridgway, can buy thee, *and keep thee !*"

The course of reading mentioned above has been imagined by many to indicate a degree of irreligion upon Girard's part, and this erroneous supposition was further fixed in the public mind by the clause in his will forbidding ministers or priests of any sect whatsoever, to either hold office in, or be admitted as visitors to, his college.[1] As a matter of fact, however, he was far from either irreligious or atheistic, having been baptized in the Roman Catholic Church, in which denomination he died, although he did not attend its services for some time prior to his death, and having many times refused to sever his connection with that Church, though often urgently solicited. He paid for, and on more than one occasion is known to have occupied, a pew in St. Augustine's Roman Catholic Church, on Crown Street above R ce, where the members of his family attended service, and from which two of his nieces were married. Each one of his apprentices was expected to go to his particular church regularly every Sunday, and this rule was enforced without exceptions, save in the case of actual

---

[1] Will, Art. XXI, § 9.

illness.[1] He gave liberally and impartially to all religious denominations worthy of such assistance, and in the government of his private life endeavored to observe the strictest moral law, in this succeeding doubtless as well as commonly falls to the lot of individual mankind. Following the custom of his native land, his day of recreation was Sunday, on which day he usually dined some friends at two o'clock in the afternoon, notably, as has been mentioned above, Joseph Buonaparte, Comte de Survilliers and ex-King of Spain and Naples, and his gentlemen.[2]

But though he never formally separated himself from the Church in which he was born, there is no doubt that his opinions underwent a very great change when brought in contact with members of the "Society of Friends" in Philadelphia, the purity of whose life and the simplicity of whose religious faith acted powerfully upon a mind readily susceptible to the virtues these external evidences made manifest. He did not hesitate to openly model his life in a great degree after their pattern, and not only felt the greatest regard for their tenets, but very warmly expressed his admiration of them as a body in a manner whose sincerity cannot be doubted.

Realizing, therefore, in his own case, the difficulty of choosing between the various religious denomina-

[1] Professor William Wagner, Lecture II.
[2] Professor William Wagner, Lecture V ; also see page 127, *supra.*

tions, he inferred, either rightly or wrongly, that a
similar choice was not one to be put upon the tender
mind of an infant; and his College being destined for
all orphaned children, irrespective of what had been
the creed of their deceased parents, it was evident that
it must perforce itself be free from any sectarian bias.
Nor would he tolerate that his intention that each
orphan should be in a position to choose for himself,
when arrived at years of discretion, should be defeated through the efforts of zealous visitors, who
might conceive their duty directed the attempt to
make converts; and the surest method of securing
this intention being the exclusion, as far as possible,
of every person who might be likely to attempt such ·
a thing, there was naturally suggested the regulation
which has attracted such universal attention.

The directions in the will upon this subject are as
follows: " I enjoin and require that no ecclesiastic,
missionary, or minister of any sect whatsoever, shall
ever hold or exercise any station or duty whatever
in the said College; nor shall any such person ever be
admitted for any purpose, or as a visitor, within the
premises appropriated to the purposes of the said
College. In making this restriction I do not mean to
cast any reflection upon any sect or person whatsoever; but as there is such a multitude of sects, and
such a diversity of opinion amongst them, I desire

to keep the tender minds of the orphans, who are to derive advantage from this bequest, free from the excitement which clashing doctrines and sectarian controversy are so apt to produce. My desire is, that all the instructors and teachers in the College shall take pains to instill into the minds of the scholars the purest principles of morality, so that on their entrance into active life they may, from inclination and habit, evince benevolence toward their fellow-creatures, and a love of truth, sobriety, and industry, adopting at the same time such religious tenets as their matured reason may enable them to prefer." [1]

It will be evident from this passage, as from the general tenor of Girard's life, that his habits of thought differed widely from those of his fellows; and it is perhaps not very surprising, since the latter failed to comprehend these, that they failed also to understand what the object was that he kept constantly before him as the single aim of his existence.

"Steady, persevering, and judicious in the pursuit of wealth, he seemed to those who could not penetrate his hidden motives to covet it for its own sake and to labor for no other purpose than to see his hoards and investments increase. The simple and economic modes of life that permitted the accumulation of the gains on which the superstructure of his fortune was built, remained comparatively unchanged when he

[1] Will, Art. XXI, § 9.

was able to count his ships by squadrons, his mansions by scores, and his moneyed capital by millions. In a country where, perhaps more than in any other, wealth seems to be chiefly desired for the *éclat* which its elegant expenditure furnishes, the character of Girard remained an enigma. It was even more inscrutable to those who saw him more nearly than others, and were aware that to an attention to business and a strict economy was added benevolence of an active description, that shunned no personal exertion or sacrifice." [1]

But to his biographers, who, having his whole life spread before them, are supposed to have given the subject an attention impossible to his fellow-citizens, the error of the supposition that his aim was the mere accumulation of wealth should have been unmistakably apparent at the outset. Indeed, to one of these it seems to have been so. "It was not the love of money," says this latter historian, "that kept him at work early and late to the last days of his life," and having come thus close upon the truth, the author unfortunately halts at the very verge of discovery, dismissing the subject with the more generous solution that Girard's chief object was forgetfulness of "early disappointments" and the unhappy chapter of his marriage.[2] He supports this latter conclusion ap arently quite strongly by two quota-

[1] *American Quarterly Review*, Vol. XIII, pp. 144 and 145.
[2] Arey, p. 23, quoted by Parton, p. 239.

tions from letters of Girard's, the first of which is as follows : " When I rise in the morning my only effort is to labor so hard during the day that when night comes I may be enabled to sleep soundly," in which sentence the author mentioned sees " a vista of disappointed hopes and broken ties " and of " misery in the midst of millions," which, as being the sincere opinion of a remarkably fair writer, is entitled to consideration.[1]

But let us see whether this construction is warranted by the facts of Girard's life. There is no known time when this remarkable man did *not* labor with the utmost assiduity. Leaving home when but fourteen years old, he commenced then a life whose whole course is well expressed in the sentence quoted, and the same argument applies with equal force against the inference from the second quotation, which latter is taken from a letter written by Girard in 1804 to his friend Duplessis, in New Orleans.

This second passage is : " I observe with pleasure that you have a numerous family, that you are happy and in the possession of an honest fortune. This is all that a wise man has the right to wish for. As to myself, I live like a galley-slave, constantly occupied, and often passing the night without sleeping. I am wrapped up in a labyrinth of affairs, and worn out

[1] Arey, p. 24.

with care. *I do not value fortune.* The love of labor is my highest ambition. You perceive that your situation is a thousand times preferable to mine.[1]

It cannot be denied that upon casual consideration this quotation seems to indicate something of the disappointment hinted at by the author, but the present writer believes, nevertheless, that a closer examination will prove it a very unsubstantial basis upon which to rest the theory that the single motive of Girard's life was a desire to forget. It is not intended to suggest that at that particular period Girard, childless at nearly sixty years of age, may not have felt his lack of issue bear heavily upon his spirits ; and the sadness of this reflection, coupled with the tinge of melancholy natural to advancing age, is quite sufficient to account for such tone of regret as the author imagines the letter unconsciously discloses. But in drawing from his quotations the inference that " the belief in childhood that he had not been given his share of the love and kindness that had been extended to others," was a fundamental motive in Girard's life, a life remarkable for its singleness of purpose, the author ascribes an importance to youthful troubles that it is not believed experience will warrant. The present writer cannot adopt the opinion that such troubles form sufficient inducement

[1] Letter to Duplessis, quoted by Arey, p. 25, also quoted by Parton, p. 239.

to lead a lad but fourteen years old to adopt a life of labor in search of forgetfulness, and while these "early disappointments" did undoubtedly, as has been hereinbefore shown, furnish the controlling motive turning his life into a particular channel, it is not believed that they proved of such permanent character as to govern his existence for any considerable length of time. Indeed, that they did not prove of lasting force is shown by the fact that notwithstanding his undeniable dislike for his stepmother, Girard frequently revisited his home during the nine years following his first departure from Bordeaux,[1] and also that he corresponded with his brother Jean [de Mombrun] during the whole of the latter's life ; that he sent to France for his nephews, sons of his brother Etienne, educating and caring for them for years ;[2] that he corresponded more or less irregularly with his father[3] and with his brother Etienne ;[4] and lastly, that all his relatives were individually left legacies in his will.

It would seem that these facts should be further sufficient to disprove the author's additional statement that Girard was " alienated from his home, his parents, and his friends," but after suggesting that it is absurd to attach importance to such juvenile friendships as Girard forsook upon leaving home at that early age,

[1] *Ante*, p. 28.   [2] *Post*, pp. 146, 147.   [3] *Ante*, pp. 40, 41.   [4] *Post*, p. 148.

the present writer is happily able to produce in refu-
tation of the remainder of the statement evidence
apparently not at the former biographer's disposal.
This is the sworn testimony taken in France, September 8th, 1839, under a commission from the United
States Circuit Court for the Eastern District of
Pennsylvania, to be used in a suit brought by one of
the heirs of Girard against the city of Philadelphia,
trustees under his will,[1] the most applicable parts
of which testimony are as follows :

(1.) The fifth witness called, M. Choury, attorney-
at-law, residing at Périgueux, testified, among other
things :

" It is publicly notorious in the city of Périgueux
and in the province, where the family of Girard originated, that Stephen Girard, who died in Philadelphia,
had left his country very young, engaged in the
French marine. *That he had constant relations with
his relatives in France*, and in particular with his
brother, Etienne Girard. That after having acquired
the considerable fortune he possessed, he had called
to him the two male children of his brother Etienne.
That he had taken care of their education, and had
given them those proofs of affection which they naturally deserve for their qualities and for their name."

[1] Vidal *vs.* The Mayor, etc , of Philadelphia. See transcript of the Records of
the U. S. Supreme Court, No. 22, Vol. II, page 85, of transcript, and page 120 of
case.

(2.) The sixth witness called, Barthélmy Michellet, President of the Tribunal of Commerce of Périgueux, confirmed the preceding, and added : " All the inhabitants of this city know *that the late Stephen Girard, of Philadelphia, had entertained for his brother Etienne and his children a particular affection.* That he had called to him the only two male children of his brother Etienne ; that he had taken care of their education, and it was thought that he destined them to continue the immense affairs to which he had initiated them from their infancy, in which direction of affairs he caused them to act as his clerks."

And (3.) The seventh witness called, Jean Baptiste Vidal, M. D., formerly Mayor of the city of Périgueux, beside additionally testifying to the above statements, added : " During the fifteen years that I performed the duties of Mayor of the city of Périgueux, I received in that capacity a letter from Mr. Stephen Girard, of Philadelphia, who informed me of his prosperous condition, and asked me information respecting his brother Etienne, who resided in Périgueux, who his family consisted of, and what were his means of existence. He manifested to me his intention of sharing with him and his children the favors which Fortune had so abundantly heaped upon him. At his request I communicated his letter to Etienne Girard. I answered Mr. Stephen Girard's letter, and a correspondence was established between the two brothers. Etienne Girard was the father of many children. He had eight children. His fortune was inconsiderable. I knew that in some instances, Mr. Stephen Girard sent to his brother and his wife some amounts of money. * * * * I have known particularly the relations entertained between the two brothers. *They were of a reciprocal good-will.*"

The writer regards the above evidence as sufficiently refuting the idea of Girard's alienation from his family; such interruption of intercourse as really took place being undoubtedly rather the effect of distance and the imperfect intercommunication of the day than of design; and considering the question of "early disappointments" thus disposed of, there remains the supposition that Girard's desire to forget the painful chapter of his later married life, was the secret of his assiduous devotion to labor. But apart from the fact that his industry was quite as marked before as after that epoch, it should be remembered that his wife's affliction was preceded by eight years of happy and contented companionship with him, which he could scarcely have wished to forget; and in addition, the writer has endeavored to show that while he mourned deeply and sincerely the terrible misfortune which had made him at once childless and worse than wifeless, his affection for the partner of his life had, happily, been of such character that he had no cause of regret as for a duty unperformed. There is, therefore, a most prominent lack of foundation in both the reasons, to wit, alienation from his friends and family and a desire to forget unhappiness, which have been advanced to explain the motive of Girard's untiring energy, a misconception on the part of the author referred to, all the more surprising in view of the closeness with which he has approached the true explanation.

What then was this great and overmastering impulse, that dominated the whole course of Girard's life and governed every act of his remarkable career? If his labor was not an endeavor to subtract something from his condition, what was the object that he sought to add?

The first definite hint of his purpose is found in a letter sent him from Cape François, Santo Domingo, by his brother Jean [de Mombrun], in which occurs the following passage: " I have just received yours of the 30th and 31st of October. It is really laughable to ask me for a method by which you can make some money. You will always be the same, never content. I dare even say you are not satisfied with this last voyage of the brig, which will certainly yield at least fifty-five thousand pounds profit. * * * * Therefore, since *I am not so ambitious as you*, if you

are not pleased with our management of your business, put it in the hands of whomsoever may seem
good to you, we will always remain friends." [1]

It is in this italicized phrase that is first given voice
the great passion that kept Girard at work not only
" early and late," but from his very boyhood down to
the last hours of a life pre-eminently crowned with its
triumph. " If we were to specify the prominent point
of his character," writes a discerning memorialist
shortly after his decease, " we should mention a
feature that would perhaps be the last that was supposed to belong to this individual—ambition. He
sought money not from avarice, but from a desire for
power. Money was the only avenue by which he
could obtain the eminence that he coveted, not money
to be dissipated in rich salons and splendid
equipages and liveried servants bearing his badge,
but wealth to be exercised as the Archimedean lever
by which he could move the fiscal world. The desire
of this, as the means of influence, was the master
spirit which conquered his soul." [2] " My deeds must
be my life. When I am dead my actions must speak
for me," was his reply to captious critics or inquisi-
tive impertinence,[3] and the fire of his ambition burned
so clear that kindred flames were stirred in the

[1] Letter of 25th of November, 1784.
[2] Anonymous article in *Hunt's Merchant's Magazine*, Vol. IV, p. 367.
[3] Said by Girard to Simpson.—Professor William Wagner, Lecture III. Also, see
American Daily Advertiser, Philadelphia, 12th January, 1832.

bosoms of those nearest to him. "The force with which I work is annihilating me," writes his brother; "I feel my strength abandoning me, so that, unless I adopt some remedy, I see my days wasting away in the pains and torments of the ambition you have aroused in me;"[1] and, again: "I do not hesitate to say, my brother, that I see with regret my days vanish without pleasure or satisfaction, on the contrary, tormented by the ambition you have waked."[2]

But the wish for money as a means of influence was a master-spirit modified by a secondary motive in his character, which, though it had always existed, had yet lain comparatively dormant until financial power enabled him to make its influence felt. The purpose for which he coveted the eminence at last attained was one quite to be expected from a native of Bordeaux, the Utopian aspirations of whose people for a voice in public affairs for many years rendered her name synonymous with Revolution. Born among and spending the whole of his young manhood amid principles of political asceticism, the entire life of Girard shows how thoroughly he had become imbued with their spirit. Simplicity of private life, coupled with untiring industry; a Cincinnatus-like readiness to sacrifice private interests

[1] Letters of Jean (de Mombrun), 8th March, 1787.
[2] Letters of Jean (de Mombrun), 17th March, 1787.

for those of a State which would secure the individual's liberty in the pursuit of happiness ; in short, the perfect example of a law-abiding citizen was the ideal of Girard's aspiration and the sole tradition he desired to leave surviving him. The long steps by which he built up the largest fortune of his day bear each one the stamp of the probity and integrity that was to be afterward unassailable. His fortune once acquired—the character of a fearless, patriotic, and, withal, humane citizen once established, he built a marble monument on such unheard-of scale and for such benevolent purpose that posterity's attention must perforce be challenged to regard its founder, a consistent purpose of whose life had been to preserve the character that could alone sustain such close inspection.

His great ambition, then, was first, success ; and this attained, the longing of mankind to leave a shining memory merged his purpose in the establishment of what was to him that fairest of Utopias—the simple tradition of a citizen. A citizen whose public duties ended not with the State, and whose benefactions were not limited to the rescue or advancement of ITS interests alone, but whose charities broadened beyond the limits of duty or the boundaries of an individual life, to stretch over long reaches of the future, enriching thousands of poor children in his beloved city

yet unborn. His life shows clearly why he worked,
as his death showed clearly the fixed object of his
labor in acquisition. " While he was forward with an
apparent disregard of self, to expose his life in behalf
of others in the midst of pestilence, to aid the internal
improvements of the country, and to promote its
commercial prosperity by all the means within his
power, he yet had more ambitious designs. He
wished to hand himself down to immortality by the
only mode that was practicable for a man in his
position, and he accomplished precisely that which
was the grand aim of his life. He wrote his epitaph
in those extensive and magnificent blocks and squares
which adorn the streets of his adopted city, in the
public works and eleemosynary establishments of
his adopted State, and erected his own monument,
and embodied his own principles in a marble-roofed
palace." [1]

" Yet, splendid as is the structure which stands
above his remains, the most perfect model of architecture in the New World, it yields in beauty to the
moral monument. The benefactor sleeps among the
orphan poor whom his bounty is constantly rearing.
Thus, forever present, unseen but felt, he daily
stretches forth his invisible hands to lead some friendless child from ignorance and vice to usefulness and

[1] *Hunt's Merchant's Magazine*, Vol. IV, p. 371.

perhaps distinction. And when, in the fullness of time, many homes have been made happy, many orphans have been fed, clothed, and educated, and many men rendered useful to their country and themselves, each happy home, or rescued child, or useful citizen, will be a living monument to perpetuate the name and embalm the memory of the dead 'Mariner and Merchant.' " [1]

[1] Arey, pp. 5 and 6.

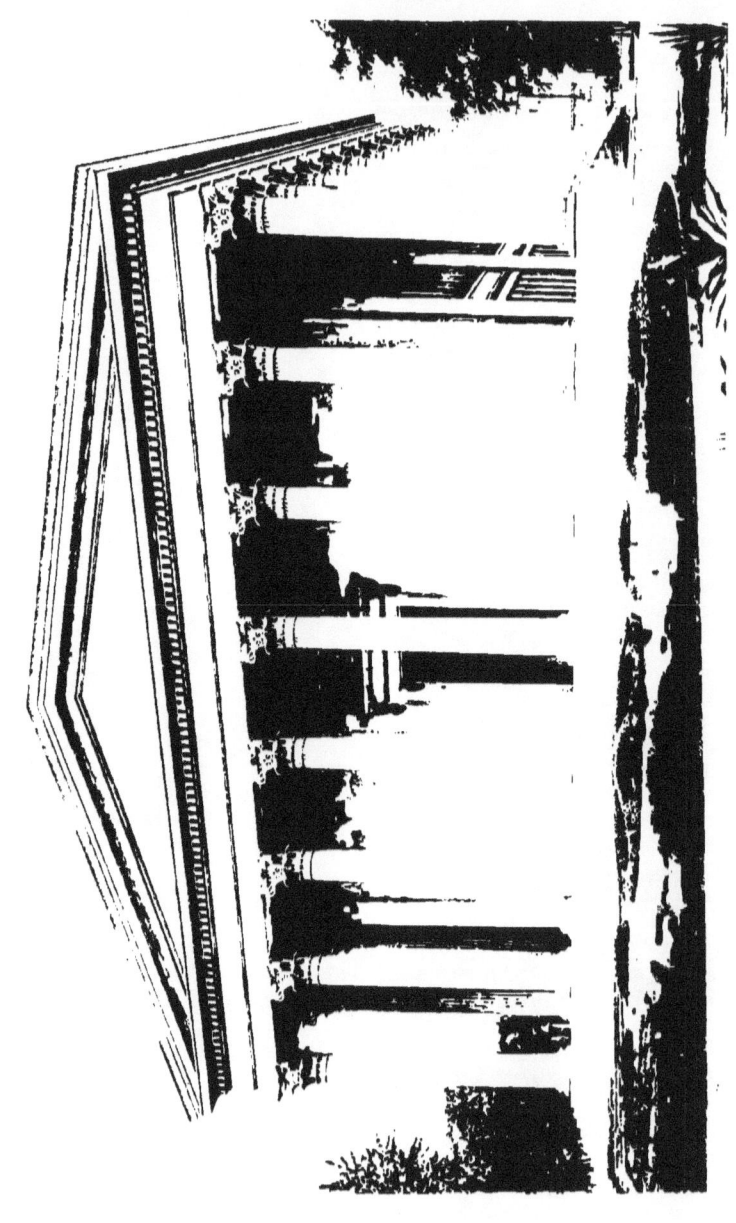

APPENDIX.[1]

THE estate of Stephen Girard amounted, at the time of his decease, to about seven millions five hundred thousands of dollars. It was the greatest fortune known in America at that day, and was surpassed by few, if by any of the private fortunes abroad. One hundred and forty thousand dollars of this was bequeathed to members of his family; sixty-five thousand as a principal sum for the payment of annuities to certain friends and former employés; one hundred and sixteen thousand to various Philadelphia charities; five hundred thousand to the city of Philadelphia, for the improvement of its Delaware waterfront; three hundred thousand to the State of Pennsylvania, for the prosecution of internal improvements, and an indefinite sum in various legacies to apprentices, sea-captains, who should bring his vessels in their charge safely to port, and to house-servants. He devised to the cities of New Orleans and Philadelphia

[1] Mainly condensed from Arey, and from the report of the architect of the Girard College. See *Journal of the Franklin Institute*, Vol. XXI, p. 354, and Vols. XXII and XXIII (New Series).

The writer is also desirous of acknowledging his indebtedness to A. H. Fetterolf, Ph. D., President of Girard College, for various information respecting the government of the Institution.

two hundred and eighty thousand acres of land in Ouachita Township, State of Louisiana (subsequently lost to the legatees by a decision of the United States Supreme Court), and all the rest, residue and remainder of his estate he devised in trust to the city of Philadelphia for the following purposes: (1) To erect, improve, and maintain a College for poor, white, orphan boys; (2) To establish a better police system; and (3) To improve the city of Philadelphia, and diminish taxation.

The sum of two millions of dollars was set apart by his will for the expense of construction of the College, and as soon as was practicable the executors appropriated certain securities, to that amount, for the purpose. Heavy depreciation in their value during the construction of the buildings, however, compelled recourse to be had to the residuary fund intended for the maintenance of the College, in order to insure their completion, the actual outlay for erection and finishing of the edifice being one million nine hundred and thirty-three thousand eight hundred and twenty-one dollars and seventy-eight cents ($1,933,821.78). Excavation was commenced May 6th, 1833, the corner-stone being laid with ceremonies on the Fourth of July following, and the completed buildings were transferred to the Board of Directors on the 13th of November, 1847. There was thus occupied in construction a period of fourteen years and six months, the work being somewhat delayed by reason of suits brought by the heirs of Girard against the estate, and the design adopted was substantially that furnished by Thomas U. Walters, an architect elected by the Board of Directors after the rejection of advertised-for competing plans. Some modifications were rendered advisable by the change of site directed in the second codicil of Girard's will, the original purpose having been to occupy the square bounded by Eleventh, Chestnut, Twelfth, and Market Streets, in the heart of the city of Philadelphia. But Girard having, subsequently to the first draft of his will, purchased for thirty-five thousand dollars[1] the William Parker farm of forty-five acres, on the Ridge Road, known as the " Peel Hall Estate," he directed that the site of his College should be transferred to that locality, and commenced the erection of stores and dwellings upon the former plot of ground, which dwellings and stores form part of his residuary estate.

The College proper closely resembles in design a Greek temple in white marble, the material for the construction of which was chiefly obtained from quarries in Montgomery and Chester Counties, Pennsylvania, and at Egremont, Massachusetts. A broad

[1] Professor William Wagner, Lecture II.

platform or stylobate, approached on every side by
eleven marble steps, supports the *cella* or main body
of the building, as also a colonnade of thirty-four
Corinthian columns, these latter forming the peristyle
and aiding in the support of the marble roof. The
cella measures one hundred and eleven feet in width,
one hundred and sixty-nine feet in length, and fifty-
nine feet eight inches in height. The columns are
six feet in diameter and fifty-five feet in height, the
diameter of the corner columns being increased one
and one-half inches in order to overcome the apparent reduction of size arising from their insulated
position. The bases are nine feet three inches in
diameter and three feet two inches high, and the capi-
tals are eight feet six inches high and nine feet four
inches wide on the face of the abacus. Each shaft
as well as the bases, consists of a single piece without
vertical joints, the total weight of each column being
one hundred and three tons and the cost twelve thousand nine hundred and ninety-four dollars.

The extreme height from the top of the columns to
the apex of the pediment is thirty-four feet, and
the elevation of the pediment is one-ninth of the
span. The whole height of the entablature, which is
enriched with a congeries of moldings and a sculp-
tured cymatium, is sixteen feet four inches. The roof
is composed of marble tiles four feet and one-half

long, four feet wide, and two and three-fourths inches
thick, the joints covered with a marble saddle hol-
lowed on the under side to embrace ridges left on the
edges of adjacent tiles. Every tile overlaps the one
below six inches, and the under side is grooved and
fitted to corresponding ridges and projections on the
surface, thus preventing the admission of water from
beating rains or capillary attraction. The tiles rest
on nine-inch brick walls. They are two thousand
and forty-six in number, the aggregate weight of the
roof being nine hundred and sixty-nine and one-half
tons, exclusive of the brick walls supporting it. The
gutters are of brick and flagstones, laid in hydraulic
cement and covered with heavy milled lead. Every
block of marble in the building is set on pieces of
milled lead, in order to prevent fracture at the joints,
and every stone is doweled into the stones above and
below and at each end, and also securely cramped to
the brick work and to the adjacent stones by means of
heavy cramp irons. The ceiling of the peristyle is of
cast iron, enriched with deep sunken panels, and, with
the balusters and skylights, is the only portion of the
building proper that is not of stone or brick. The
floor of the peristyle is of white marble accurately
jointed, and the thrust of the interior arches forming
the roof and floors is taken up by five huge chains of
wrought iron, completely encircling the *cella* and built

into the masonry of its walls at various heights from
the base. The building covers an area of thirty-four
thousand three hundred and forty-four superficial feet,
exclusive of the steps, the total weight being seventy-
six thousand five hundred and ninety four and one-
half tons, and the average weight resolved on each
superficial foot of foundation being about six tons.

The building is three stories in height, the first and
second being twenty-five feet from floor to floor, and
the third thirty feet in the clear to the eye of the
dome, the doors of entrance being in the north and
south fronts, and measuring sixteen feet in width and
thirty-two in height. The walls of the *cella* are four
feet in thickness, and are pierced on each flank by
twenty windows. At each end of the building is a
vestibule, extending across the whole width of the
cella, the ceilings of which are supported on each
floor by eight columns, whose shafts are composed of
a single stone. Those on the first floor are Ionic,
from the temple on the Illusus, at Athens; on
the second, a modified Corinthian, from the Tower
of Andronicus Cyrrhestes, also at Athens, and on
the third, a similar modification of the Corinthian,
somewhat lighter and more ornate. In each vestibule two flights of "geometric stairs" lead to
the floor above, these stairs having one end of
each step built into the wall, and the lower edge

of each supported by the step below, thus doing away with the necessity of support for the outer end. The whole of these steps, columns, and floors is of white marble, the floor-tiles being accurately jointed to prevent loosening. Each floor is divided into four rooms, each fifty feet square, vaulted with brick, those of the first and second stories having groined arches, and those of the third story pendentive domes springing from the floors. The reverberation of sound in these rooms caused by their arched ceiling is obviated by false ceilings of canvas stretched over a light wooden frame.

The building, including the vestibules, the cellars, and the space under the exterior steps, is warmed by means of steam, and each room is ventilated by registers, which open from near the ceiling into the main flues.

There are ten auxiliary buildings, including a handsome Gothic chapel of white marble, dormitories, offices and laundries, four of them having been constructed under the directions of the will, and the others having been added from time to time as necessity arose. These are faced with marble and roofed with copper, slate, or tin, the stairways in the four original dormitories being of marble, with wrought-iron balustrades, and those in the buildings subsequently added, of iron and slate. A new refectory, containing improved ranges and steam cooking apparatus, has recently been added, the dining-hall of which will seat with ease more than one thousand persons. A bathing pool in the western portion of the grounds affords amusement to the pupils, and a well sixteen feet in diameter, the water from which is forced by means of a steam engine into four iron tanks or reservoirs, supplies the water used in the Institution. The outbuildings are heated by steam, and the whole Institution is lighted by gas obtained from the city works. A wall sixteen inches in thickness and ten feet in height, strengthened by spur piers on the inside and capped with marble coping, surrounds the whole estate, its length being six thousand eight hundred and forty-three feet, or somewhat more than one and one-quarter miles. It is pierced on the southern side, immediately facing the south front of the main building, for the chief entrance, this last being flanked by two octagonal white marble lodges, between which stretches an ornamental wrought-iron *grille*, with wrought-iron gates, the whole forming an approach in keeping with the large simplicity of the College itself.

The site upon which this latter is erected corresponds well with its splendor and importance. It is elevated considerably above the general level of the surrounding buildings, and forms a conspicuous object, not only from the higher windows and roofs in every part of Philadelphia, but from the Delaware River many miles below the city, and from eminences far out in the country. From the lofty marble roof (to which access is so easy that almost every visitor ascends) the view is also exceedingly beautiful, embracing the city and its environs for many miles around, and the course, to their confluence, eight miles below, of both those noble rivers which enclose the Quaker City.

The history of the Institution commences shortly after the decease of Girard, when the Councils of Philadelphia, acting as his trustees, elected a Board of Directors, which organized on the 18th of February, 1833, with Nicholas Biddle as Chairman. A Building Committee was also appointed by the City Councils on the 21st of the following March, in whom was vested the immediate supervision of the construction of the College, an office in which they continued without in-termission until the final completion of the structure.

On the 19th of July, 1836, the former body, having previously been authorized by the Councils so to do, proceeded to elect Alexander Dallas Bache President of the College, and instructed the latter to visit various similar institutions in Europe, purchasing the necessary books and apparatus for the school, both of which he did, making an exhaustive report upon his return in 1838. It was then attempted to establish schools without awaiting the completion of the main building, but competent legal advice being unfavorable to the organization of the Institution prior to that time, the idea was surrendered, and difficulties having meanwhile arisen between the Councils and the Board of Directors, the ordinances creating the Board and authorizing the election of the President were repealed.

In June, 1847, a new Board was appointed, to whom the buildings were transferred, and on December 15th, 1847, the officers of the Institution were elected, the Hon. Joel Jones, President Judge of the District Court for the City and County of Philadelphia, being chosen as President. On January 1st, 1848, the College was opened with a class of one hundred orphans, previously admitted, the occasion being signalized by appropriate ceremonies. On October 1st of the same year one hundred more were admitted, and on April 1st, 1849, an additional one hundred, since when others have been admitted as vacancies have occurred, or to swell the number as facilities have increased. The College now (1884) contains upward of eleven hundred pupils.

On June 1st, 1849, Judge Jones resigned the office of President of the College, and on the 23d of the following November William H. Allen, LL. D., Professor of Mental Philosophy and English Literature in Dickinson College, was elected to fill the vacancy. He was installed January 1st, 1850, but resigned December 1st, 1862, and Major Richard Somers Smith was recalled from active service in the United States Army to fill his place. Major Smith was inaugurated June 24th, 1863, and resigned in September, 1867, Dr. Allen being immediately re-elected and continuing in office until his death, on the 29th of August, 1882.

The present incumbent, A. H. Fetterolf, Ph. D. (Lafayette), was elected December 27th, 1882, by the Board of Directors, the members of which body are no longer elected by the Councils, but appointed by the Judges of the Courts of Common Pleas of the City of Philadelphia. The Board has a membership of fifteen, twelve of whom are appointed for life, the number being completed by three Directors *ex-officio*, viz.: The Mayor of the city of Philadelphia and the respective Presidents of the Select and Common Councils. Its meetings are held on the second Wednesday of each month.

It has been determined by the Courts of Pennsylvania that any child having lost its father is properly denominated an orphan, irrespective of whether the mother be living or not.[1] This construction has

[1] Soohan *vs.* Philadelphia, reported in 1 Grant's Cases 505, and in 9 Casey 20.

been adopted by the College, the requirements for admission to the Institution being as follows : (1) The orphan must be a white male, between six and ten years of age, no application for admission being received before the former age, nor can he be admitted into the College after passing his tenth birthday, even though the application has been made previously; (2) the mother or next friend is required to produce the marriage certificate of the child's parents (or, in its absence, some other satisfactory evidence), and also the certificate of the physician setting forth the time and place of birth; (3) a form of application looking to the establishment of the child's identity, physical condition, morals, previous education, and means of support, must be filled in, signed, and vouched for by respectable citizens. Applications are made the first Monday of each month, at the office, No. 19 South Twelfth Street, Philadelphia, between the hours of nine and twelve A. M.

A preference is given under Girard's will to (*a*) orphans born in the city of Philadelphia; (*b*) those born in any other part of Pennsylvania; (*c*) those born in the city of New York ; (*d*) those born in the city of New Orleans. The preference to the orphans born in the city of Philadelphia is defined to be strictly limited to the old city proper, the districts subsequently consolidated into the city having no rights in this respect over any other portion of the State.

Orphans are admitted, in the above order, strictly according to priority of application, the mother executing an indenture binding the orphan to the city of Philadelphia, as trustee under Girard's will, as an orphan to be educated and provided for by the College. The scholars are fed, clothed, and taught wholly by the Institution. No distinctive dress is ever to be worn; and although the orphans reside permanently in the College, they are, at stated times, allowed to visit friends at the latter's houses and to receive visits from their friends at the College The household is under the care of a matron, an assistant matron, twelve prefects, and fourteen governesses, who superintend the moral and social training of the orphans and administer the discipline of the Institution when the scholars are not in the school-rooms. The pupils are divided into sections for the purposes of discipline, which last have distinct officers, buildings, and playgrounds.

The schools are conducted principally, though not entirely, in the main College building, four professors and thirty-one teachers being employed in the duties of instruction, and the course comprises a thorough English commercial education, to which has been latterly added special schools of technical instruction in the mechanical arts. As a large proportion of the orphans admitted into the College have had little or no preparatory education, the instruction commences with the alphabet, and includes during the first year, spelling, reading, writing, drawing (on slates), primary arithmetic, and object lessons.

The order of daily exercises is as follows: The pupils rise at six o'clock, take breakfast at half-past six. Recreation until half-past seven; then assemble in the section rooms at that hour, and proceed to the Chapel for morning worship at eight. The Chapel exercises consist of singing a hymn, reading a chapter from the Old or New Testament, and prayer, after the conclusion of which the pupils proceed to the various school-rooms, where they remain, with a recess of fifteen minutes, until twelve. From twelve until the dinner-hour, which is half-past twelve, they are on the playground, returning there after finishing that meal, until two o'clock, the afternoon school-hour, when they resume the school exercises, remaining, without intermission, until four o'clock. At four the afternoon service in the Chapel is held, after which they are on the playground until six, at which hour supper is served. The evening study hour lasts from seven to eight, or half-past eight, varying with the age of the pupils, the same difference being observed in their bedtimes, which are from half-past seven for the youngest until a quarter before nine.

On Sunday the pupils assemble in their section rooms at nine o'clock in the morning, and at two in the afternoon for religious reading and instruction, and at half-past ten o'clock in the morning, and at three in the afternoon, they attend Divine worship in the Chapel. Here the exercises are similar to those held on weekdays, with the important addition of an appropriate discourse adapted to the comprehension of the pupils, which last is delivered either by the President of the College or by some other layman selected by him for the purpose. The services in the Chapel, whether on Sunday or on weekdays, are invariably conducted by the President or other selected layman, the will of the founder forbidding the entrance of clergymen of any denomination whatsoever within the boundaries of the Institution.

The discipline of the College is almost entirely administered through admonition, deprivation of recreation, and seclusion; but in extreme cases corporal punishment may be inflicted by order of the President and in his presence. If by reason of misconduct a pupil becomes an unfit companion for the rest, the right to dismiss him summarily is vested in the Board of Directors.

The annual cost per capita of maintaining, clothing,

8

and educating each pupil, including current repairs to buildings and furniture and the maintenance of the grounds, is about three hundred and twelve dollars, and those scholars who merit it remain in the College until between fourteen and eighteen years of age, at the discretion of the Board. Between these ages they are indentured by the Institution, on behalf of " The City of Philadelphia," to learn some " art, trade, or mystery," until their twenty-first year, consulting, as far as is judicious, the inclination and preference of the scholar. The master to whom an apprentice is bound agrees to furnish the latter with sufficient meat, drink, apparel, washing, and lodging at his own place of residence (unless otherwise agreed to by the parties to the indenture and so indorsed upon it) ; to use his best endeavors to teach and instruct the apprentice in his " art, trade, or mystery," and at the expiration of the apprenticeship to furnish him with at least two complete suits of clothes, one of which shall be new. Should a scholar not be apprenticed by the Institution, however, he must leave the College upon attaining the age of eighteen years, and in case of death his friends have the privilege of removing his body for interment, though should this not be preferred, his remains are placed in the College burial-lot at Laurel Hill Cemetery, near Philadelphia.

Citizens and strangers provided with a permit

are allowed to visit the College on the afternoon of every weekday. Permits can be obtained from the Mayor of Philadelphia, at his office, on the southwest corner of Fifth and Chestnut Streets, Philadelphia ; from a Director; at the office of the Board of City Trusts, No. 19 South Twelfth Street, Philadelphia ; or at the office of the *Public Ledger* newspaper, on the southwest corner of Sixth and Chestnut Streets, Philadelphia. It is to be observed, however, that the passes obtained from the *Public Ledger* office will not admit visitors on Fridays, that being the " Battalion drill day," and it having been found that the central position of the *Ledger* office was likely to result in the issuance of so many passes for that day as to seriously interfere with the exercises. Especial courtesy is shown all foreign visitors, and particularly to those interested in educational matters, in whose favor the rigidity of the above rules is invariably relaxed upon proper application either to a Director or to the President of the College, at his office in the College buildings.

THE END.

INDEX.

(The abbreviation *App.* signifies *Appendix.*)

173

www.ingramcontent.com/pod-product-compliance
Lightning Source LLC
Chambersburg PA
CBHW030607040726
47497CB00008B/2883